Gary Ludwig

Basket Road Press
BRP

The Angels and Demons of Hamlin

Basket Road Press
Harrisburg, PA USA

First Edition

To order additional books contact:
info@basketroadpress.com

Acknowledgments

I continue to be grateful to all who offer encouragement. Writing can be an awful lonely existence.

To editor Heather Shumaker: all authors need a good editor. Heather used her accomplished editing skills to refine the manuscript and help make it a book.

To Joanne Thomas: her efficient composition know-how and excellent interior design talents resulted in an attractive, readable book.

To Beth Ludwig: my wife and assistant. Her administrative, logistical and research services have always been invaluable to my work. She made sure the project went forward.

The account of General John Reynolds and Catherine Hewitt is true.

I have taken the liberty to use factual data from *The Reminiscences of Carl Schurz*, Volume 3, 1908, The McClure Company, to paraphrase General Schurz's quotes and descriptions while writing my fictionalized account of his performance during The Battle of Gettysburg. His actions and dialogue following the battle that are portrayed in this book are purely fictional.

To Christine and Daniel.

To the coming of
Elijah.

In memory of Marcia and John,
Mom and Dad.

To Beth;
You're always on my mind.

Chapter 1

1819

Ephriam is born and pointed in the right direction

Henry Bernharter, the tall, balding and lanky village blacksmith of Hamlin, Pennsylvania, lingered outside on a bitter cold February night as his wife Sally labored to give birth. At forty-three years of age he had given up becoming a father, but then God blessed the couple. He kept pacing the length of the massive covered porch of his stately white frame house. It stood two blocks East of the village square along the dirt main street, often described by postmaster Jake Waller as being "always scattered with horse shit and bordered by immense chestnut trees with their branches hanging over the street, shading the entire village." Looking at the house with its large pillars holding up that mighty porch roof made you quickly aware how much wood it took to build the place. Years later it was described as a mansion, but in 1819 it was just a big wooden house, one of two dozen or so in Hamlin, with yellowing white paint peeling at the corners and edges. Inside it wasn't anything fancy; it had a cook stove in the kitchen, a potbelly stove in the parlor, and assorted pieces of furniture on oil-cloth floors. Some rugs were scattered about.

Sally was enduring her condition on a thick, massive bed in one of the chilly second floor bedrooms.

Henry's Aunt Pearl had been summoned to assist the midwife, Margaret Starkman, who made the trek from her house in the next town of Franklinsburg, only two miles North. The first thing Pearl did after arriving was to order Henry out of the house.

He walked West for a block to the center of the village, glad to be out of range of his wife's screams, then traipsed back, again within earshot of her cries. The thick cold winter air muffled the sounds that extended out through the closed windows. The screams seemed to be loud enough to be coming out of the chimney, the strong wood smelling smoke carrying them through the air to an audience of barren trees and nestled, sleeping wildlife.

His was a real life portrayal of a jittery husband, bundled up in his heavy coat, gloves, scarf, and knitted cap. The heavy clothing didn't completely stop his shivering, but the discomfort did divert some of his anxiety. He was the son of a clergyman, had been a sensitive child, and it seemed because of that he was more concerned about his wife's situation than most men of that era. He knew the pain of childbirth was natural, but he felt guilty putting Sally through it.

All the second thoughts that had haunted him the past nine months were now returning to do him more harm. He couldn't help but think they should have stopped trying to have a child. Some had suggested they might be too old to take on the responsibility; perhaps they were right. And there was so much that could go wrong; Sally could die, or the baby could be born seriously ill or afflicted.

When he made his second stroll to the village square he walked a little farther to the church at the West end and knelt at the altar rail and prayed, drawing on his faith for assurance and courage.

It had been difficult for Sally. She was unable to get out

of bed for the last two weeks of the pregnancy. She had always been a short plump girl, brown hair and eyes; now she was thirty-five years old and had gained forty pounds while carrying the child. Finally, 9 hours after the midwife had arrived, Sally's crying out stopped.

Henry now remembered how quiet winter nights could be, but he didn't think this night should be as quiet as it had suddenly become; it could only mean something went wrong! Then he thought he heard a baby's cries, so he raced into the house.

He ran through the big dimly lit foyer, up the steps, and stood still at the top of the stairwell, swaying slightly from side to side, crouching slightly to hurry a retreat, clutching his cap with both hands. He didn't take off his coat; if there were trouble he would need it when he ran outside and into the dark fields to escape dealing with any tragedy he brought about. His eyes were riveted to the door, all set to behold the smile of joy or tears of sadness on the face of whichever woman opened the bedroom door.

It was Aunt Pearl; her face wore a broad smile. Sally had given birth to a baby boy! Henry leaned over to kiss his wife on the forehead and then watched his son suck on her breast, getting his first taste of nourishment. Tears of joy from Henry's steel gray eyes rolled down his weather beaten face. The birth of their first child gave them a wonderful feeling of fulfillment. After kissing her again, Henry spoke softly, "He'll be called Ephriam."

Henry was a stern Pennsylvania German who had now been working for over twenty-five years as a blacksmith. Like his neighbors and large extended family, he spoke mostly using the area's German dialect. He was a religious man; prayer was a part of his life. He and Sally never failed to thank God when a blessing came their way. His father, Luther Bernharter, was the Lutheran minister serving St. Luke's Lutheran Church for the past thirty-two years, the same church Henry sought solace in the night of his son's birth. Luther preached mostly in formal German, not the dialect, but he also held church services in English. He and his wife Rachel had hoped Henry would also pursue the ministry, possibly taking over the church after Luther retired. Henry, however, flourished when he did physical labor. He didn't do well in school. Instead of paying attention to his lessons, he daydreamed staring out the schoolhouse window wishing he were leading a team of horses pulling a plow or hay wagon. Since Luther was a wise man and a good father, he encouraged his son to work hard pursuing and accomplishing his goals, whatever they happened to be.

Henry became an apprentice blacksmith, learning the trade while working under Dutch Landis. Landis had his blacksmith shop in back of the big white wood frame house. Twenty-two years later Dutch went to bed one night and never woke up. Henry and Sally, who had been renting a small apartment on the second floor of the general store in the village square, gladly agreed to buy the house and shop from Dutch's widow. The blacksmith shop continued to be profitable, and Henry and Sally lived a happy and comfortable life in the house.

Although he was a successful businessman, Henry did sometimes feel that he missed his calling. By the time baby Ephriam was born he sometimes wished his father had insisted he go to seminary. He came to believe that young men don't have the maturity to make decisions about their future and that fathers should decide. On that cold night, before Ephriam left his birthing bed, Henry had his son's life all planned. He would be ordained a Lutheran minister and become pastor of St. Luke's Lutheran Church in Hamlin, Pennsylvania!

Henry began taking him to the blacksmith shop as soon as the boy was old enough to walk, an early part of the plan to teach him that a man's ability to perform hard physical labor was a reinforcement of the character of an educated man, a reader of the classics, an appreciator of art and music, a man who was destined to be an important leader of his community.

Ephriam began his education at home when Sally and her mother, Maggie Auchenbach, began reading to him. He sat quietly listening to the stories of bunny rabbits, puppies, and cats chasing the mouse. He began pointing to the words and then recognizing them. When he exhibited typical little boy behavior, squirming and attempting to escape their laps, their firm clutches to restrain him were very effective.

In June 1820 Sally gave birth to a baby girl; she was named Anne. She became a beautiful child with sparkling blue eyes and long, almost white blonde hair. After so many years living a childless marriage, Henry and Sally were now blessed with two children.

Chapter 2

1825

Ephriam starts school

In the fall of 1825 Ephriam started to attend school. He was a good-looking boy with brown curly hair, brown eyes and a faultless nose on an ideal face with emerging classical features. He was athletic as well as academic with an above average interest and matching ability in reading. Due to his mother and grandmother's persistence he was able to read English and German a year before he entered first grade, which is when Henry began buying him books and taking over supervising his reading. Later he began sending him to his grandfather's house many evenings during the school term, and most mornings during the summer to the church office for tutoring and scrutiny. Reverend Bernharter insisted on book reports, as well as written and oral examinations.

Hamlin's one room schoolhouse, a building barely inhabitable, had been built with old bricks and logs from a house that collapsed after an underground stream washed out its foundation. The school was cold and damp in winter, the big windows along the walls allowing every steady wind, and even a slight breeze to enter. The undersized potbelly stove never kept the room comfortable on bitter cold days.

The schoolboys were charged with keeping the fire going, bringing inside the logs they chopped from the timber left by the neighborhood men. Occasionally a farmer, traveling north to the coal regions to deliver some corn meal or chickens, would bring back a small pile of coal that fell from a breaker's trough. The manager, not having to shovel it back into the bin, would gladly sell it for a few cents. The farmer's donation made life easier for the boys, at least for a while. Carrying a bucket of coal from outside was easier than chopping wood covered with frozen mold.

It was twenty-one-year-old Hilda Noll's first year teaching. She moved to Hamlin from the next county and boarded with a family in the nearby town of Benton, about three miles to the East. Hilda was a beautiful young woman with blue eyes, a perfect nose, and sensuous lips. She always wore her dark brown hair pulled back in a bundle and dressed in fashionable plain dresses that reached to the floor, complemented with a colorful knit sweater, or sometimes a shawl. It was Ephriam's first experience at being in love, an impossible love for a much older woman. He fantasized how it would be to be grown up and have her as his wife. Early on Hilda recognized that Ephriam was her best student and always willing to help other students, especially the younger ones. He enjoyed tutoring, and his classmates looked up to him because he was smart and willing to help.

His best friend Tommy Hertzog also wanted to marry Miss Noll. They began taunting each other but soon realized they weren't rivals for her affection. The both realized there was no chance she would wait until they grew up and then choose to marry one of them. Ephriam would continue having strong feelings toward Miss Noll, but he eventually turned his attention to two of the prettiest girls at the school. Eileen Randle and Janice Hull both returned the attention. But he would trade all the attention those two girls gave him for just one "Ephriam, I think I love you" from Miss Noll. Or

"Ephriam, I'll wait for you, I promise." Since he was pre-oc-cupied daydreaming about Miss Noll, he refused to choose between Eileen and Janice, and soon both lost interest in him. He mentioned to his mother that he couldn't understand how two girls that liked him now hate him. Sally laughed. "Son, those girls don't hate you. Someday you'll understand that a scorned woman is almost always very unkind!"

One of the other girls Ephriam had started school with was Catherine Witters. She too was one of the prettiest girls in Ephriam's class. Her parents were close friends of Henry and Sally; they owned the general store on the square. As a result of frequent visiting, Ephriam and Catherine were together when their parents were. The Witter's friendship with the Bernharters was so solid that they converted from a conservative Brethren church to the Lutheran faith so they could attend church and hear Reverend Bernharter preach. However, Catherine's mother continued to wear the tradi-tional white mesh bonnet and plain and simple dresses that the Brethren women wore, even after the family's conver-sion. Practically all the boys in school wanted to be Cath-erine's boyfriend, which made Ephriam jealous. He believed because he knew her longer than the other boys she should give him more attention. The jealousy showed, and soon Catherine had enough of his moping. She said, "If you want to be my boyfriend just say so!"

Ephriam and Catherine held hands and stole an occasion-al kiss until the beginning of eighth grade. The end of eighth grade would be catching up to Ephriam soon enough. Henry would be enrolling him at Swatara Academy, located in the next town of Jenkinstown, about five miles to the West.

Henry had told his son early on that he would be sent away to a private school. "Swatara Academy will prepare you for higher education, you'll arrive at seminary fully pre-pared to learn to preach God's Word, lead the weak and lost souls to salvation, to be a true shepherd for Jesus Christ."

Ephriam came to realize that his father had lofty aspirations built on heaps of great expectations. He wasn't nearly as enthused about becoming a minister, but he felt that he had time to prepare if he chose to become a failure in his father's eyes. He knew that if he balked at the idea of entering seminary, or after graduating, turn down ordination and decide not to preach, it would devastate his father. For now he planned to be a normal young boy and have some fun before being subjected to the repressed life at Swatara Academy.

Janice Hull turned out to be a great source of fun. She was a lot more fun than Catherine, who was influenced by her conservative parents. Janice decided to give Ephriam a second chance. She was an insecure girl; she believed the only way she could keep boys interested in her was to offer them sex. Ephriam, being a healthy young boy, wasn't going to pass up any opportunities, even knowing there would be serious consequences if his father were ever told he was taking Janice into the broom closet during recess.

Of course Tommy was jealous and did everything he could to remind Ephriam how sinful he was. "Your daddy'll lick you if he finds out what you're doing with her." Ephriam knew jealousy when he saw and heard it. "You shouldn't worry about what I do, you're not going to tell anyone, anyhow, so why not hold your tongue!"

Janice didn't hesitate to take off her clothing and hear Ephriam tell her how beautiful her body was. He got to look close-up, and he got to do what Tommy didn't get to do; Ephriam got to kiss a girl. Ephriam and Janice never did get caught.

As the time for Ephriam's enrollment in Swatara Academy got closer, Reverend Mark Randolph, who succeeded Ephriam's retiring grandfather as St. Luke's minister, cautioned Henry. "The boy must want to do it, and he'll have to receive a calling from God before he can study for the ministry. Before he can be ordained and preach the Word, he'll have to hear that call from within himself." Henry knew that. His terse response brought out all the stubbornness that was a significant part of his character. "I'll encourage him, and if I have to, I'll prod him; he needs to live the life that I should be living. I owe him that." Randolph was very concerned; he now believed Henry's dream of the life he wanted for his son had become a scary obsession, and that serious strife would result from any resistance by Ephriam.

Henry's coldness and the strict disciplining of his son was a part of the conservative Pennsylvania German culture that existed during the nineteenth century. This same culture didn't allow a wife to be critical of her husband. Sally was grateful for Henry's most important trait - devotion. His devotion to her, Ephriam, and Anne was unwavering. He worked hard to make her comfortable and to give the children opportunity. A good education for Ephriam had always topped this list. She worried though, like Reverend Randolph, that Ephriam preaching from the pulpit was more to Henry than hope. Sally didn't care what her son did with his life. She only wished that he be healthy and happy, make an honest living, and find a wife and be blessed with children.

Sally invited Hilda Noll for supper to commemorate the end of the final year she would have Ephriam as a student. She would miss him, not only because of the help he gave her tutoring, but because he was becoming a scholar, a true inspiration to her, and a proud achievement. After Ephriam and Anne were excused from the table, Hilda made a bold statement. "I should tell both of you that Ephriam is brilliant; he must always be given every opportunity to continue his studies." Henry held back, giving a measured response. He didn't want to take all the credit for his son's excellence. He saved himself from criticism by adding how Sally gave the boy the nurturing that only a mother can give, developing his self-confidence. Hilda was aware of Henry's ego. "Mr. Bernharter, Ephriam has often mentioned to me that he works very hard because he knows it will make you proud of him."

She asked if they would object to Ephriam doing private tutoring during the summer. "Some of my students will be coming to my home for reading improvement this summer. He would be very helpful working with them." Henry and Sally agreed to Hilda Noll's idea. They were proud that an educated schoolteacher thought so highly of their son.

Ephriam hadn't expected the offer; he welcomed any opportunity for a job that would keep him from working in the blacksmith shop or helping his mother do "women's work." However, Ephriam's primary motivation for wanting to tutor was to be near Miss Noll. Every morning during that summer he anxiously walked to her house, making sure he got there a half hour before the children. He wanted the chance to spend time with her before she shared herself with the students. He wanted her all to himself for those precious 30 minutes each day. The sight of her house, the sweet smell of lilacs in her front yard, the colorful red and yellow roses with their thorny branches wrapped around the trellis hovering over the walkway – his day was always brightened. He would knock on the screen door and listen to her sweet voice call out for him to come in. In the summer she wore cotton summer dresses with bright colors and flowery prints, not the thick drab skirts and plain white blouses under those bulky sweaters she wore in the classroom. Neither did she wear those ugly black old lady shoes during the summer!

On one particularly hot July day she offered him some lemonade. It was while she poured some for him and herself that he discovered she was barefoot! He never thought he would ever see her barefoot! He thought she had the most beautiful feet any woman could ever have. He really didn't realize how much he loved her until he saw her walk about the house in such a carefree way.

"Ephriam, you can take your shoes and socks off; it's so

hot, it might make you cooler." He gladly took her up on her suggestion. If only Tommy Hertzog could see him now!

One morning she called out, "Ephriam, there are some cookies in the kitchen. Help yourself. I just got out of my bath. I'll be out soon." He pretended that she baked the oatmeal cookies just for him.

She walked down the hallway with a large towel wrapped around her and into the kitchen to make sure he found the cookies. "Do you like them? It's the first time I ever baked oatmeal cookies; I remember you saying they were your favorite." Then she went into her bedroom to get dressed.

He smiled as he chewed. The smile was one of satisfaction. She actually baked them just for him!

She called out, "Ephriam, would you mind dumping my bath water?" He walked back to the utility room and dragged the tub to the door, spilling it outside into the gravel drain ditch. When he passed her bedroom door he couldn't resist kneeling down and looking through the keyhole. She hadn't dressed yet; she was standing in front of the mirror using her powder puff. The strong but pleasant lavender fragrance of the talcum was very familiar to him. He had smelled it all during his school years when she would walk up the classroom aisles, enveloping him with the wonderful scent as she passed by.

It was the day he got to see her naked, each turn she took allowed him to see more of her body. He wanted to boast that he was the only boy in school who saw Miss Noll naked, but describing the experience to Tommy Herzog and some of the other boys would dishonor her; it was bad enough he violated her by peeking through the keyhole, but that was very necessary.

Chapter 3

1833

Ephriam discovers he has a special gift

During the summer before he was to start attending Swatara Academy, Ephriam had a traumatic experience while attending the annual Sunday school picnic.

Every year hundreds of people came to the church grove, a thickly wooded acre in the back of the church building. Wooden pavilions with long picnic tables were built years earlier, and a small stage gave the area brass bands a platform to perform. People brought their kitchen chairs, moving them from area to area while they participated in the day's activities. Morning church services started the day's events, and the picnic concluded with an evening worship service.

It was a very special annual event. Extended families used it as their yearly reunion, old friends reunited, and children made new friends. While the women were busy preparing and serving the food the men got to talk planting, livestock prices, the upcoming harvest, and other business.

Families brought food to be shared with others, mostly salads and a seemingly endless variety of pies, cakes, and puddings. The small kitchen building, staffed by men and women on the picnic committee, was used to make chicken soup, corn on the cob, chicken, ribs, and steaks for every-body, plus two or three pigs were roasted over an open-pit, potatoes were baked on open fires, and gallons of lemonade and homemade ice cream were served.

Later in the day the older men tossed horseshoes, played cards, and shucked and ate oysters.

The younger men played ball games and ran foot races while the women organized games for the children.

The young women waited anxiously all day for the eve-ning dance, and as the guitar player and fiddler performed, they waited some more for that one particular shy boy to ask them to dance.

Ephriam had been running in foot races all day and eating plenty of food needed to fuel all the energy he was spending.

He was resting, deciding to spend a few minutes with his mother and sister and to eat some ice cream, when he noticed a young man, about the same age he was, sitting at the edge of the grove in an old rickety wooden wheelchair, separated from everyone else. He looked sad; he obviously didn't want to be at the picnic. Whenever Ephriam saw a handicapped person, his first reaction was to feel guilty for enjoying his good health. He wondered how sad this young boy must feel missing out on all of the running and jumping that the other boys were enjoying.

"Mother, who is that boy?" Sally would expect her son to be curious, not like the other children who were too preoccu-pied to worry about someone less fortunate. "He's from the orphanage. The people there felt it would be good for him to get fresh air and meet people. His mother abandoned him when she found out he was a cripple."

Ephriam walked over to him and introduced himself. Johnny Erman was glad to have somebody to talk to. "I didn't want to come but they made me." Ephriam had some questions to ask. "Do you have to do work there to earn your keep?" Johnny laughed. "That would be a good thing if I could work, all I do is sit and look out the window all day until it's time to go to bed. The place is very boring; the people that work there don't spend any time with us. The only time we get any treats or attention is when people from the churches visit us."

"When did you find out you couldn't move your legs?" Johnny wasn't too anxious to talk about his crippled twisted legs. "I just don't have any strength in my legs; up until I was about four years old I could walk, but I couldn't stay standing. I'd fall down all the time, and then I couldn't move my legs at all. That's when my mother dropped me off."

Ephriam asked, "Do you try to walk yourself, I mean, I think I would if I was you." Johnny turned serious. "That's easy for you to say. You can run. You don't have a worry in the world."

Ephriam could understand Johnny's bitterness and resentment. "Can I get you anything?" Johnny responded, "Sure, get that blanket over there and lay it over my legs." When he bent over and placed the blanket on Johnny's lap the back of his hand brushed against his knee. Ephriam received a violent jolt, causing him to quickly straighten up and fall backwards, backpedaling to keep from falling on his behind. His heart was fluttering, skipping beats. He was short of breath, gasping for air; his lungs felt as if all the air had been sucked out of them. He had never had an experience like that before. He was scared. He wondered if there was something terribly wrong with him. He turned and looked at Johnny, whose jaw had dropped, startled by Ephriam's sudden movement. "You don't need to worry, you won't catch anything just because you touched me, I am not a leper." Ephriam, still startled as well, reacted, "It has nothing to do with you, it's me. Just forget it happened. Something must be wrong with me."

Ephriam sat down on the ground, holding his head in his hands, trying to regain his composure. Evidently he had some medical condition that was going to cause his early death. His heart was going to beat faster and faster until it exploded!

Soon the shock of what happened with Johnny wore off somewhat. He hadn't fully recovered from the fear of dying, but enough to spend some time pushing Johnny around in the wheelchair, navigating the bumpy picnic grove terrain a lot faster than he should have been. Johnny was laughing, holding on while bouncing up and down, back and forth, and side to side, nearly launched out the front and into the air more that once. Johnny Erman hadn't had that much fun in a long time.

Later Janice walked along and soon suggested that she and Ephriam take a walk. Ephriam knew what that meant. Johnny said, "Don't worry about me; go spend some time with your girlfriend." Ephriam scanned the grove, zeroing in on his father stacking wood for the fireplaces. As long as Henry was busy he wouldn't be keeping a watchful eye on his son. He told Janice, "Go down by the creek, I'll meet you there." Janice hurried off and anxiously waited for him.

With the opportunity to be with Janice at hand, it was easy to be convinced that sinning with her was excusable because he was going to have a short life and never get married. Nobody would blame him for pursuing lustful desire when they realized he was going to be lying in the church's cemetery before he even got out of school! Why was God being so unfair? His early death was going to be very tragic, and everyone was certainly going to miss him. It was going to be especially tragic for his mother, father, and sister Anne.

He and Janice took a long walk until they were far enough away from the picnic grove to sit down on some thick grass under a big weeping Willow tree. The long thin leaves hung low, touching the ground, creating a thick green curtain. Separating them to get under the tree reminded Ephriam of a fancy Chinese bamboo curtain of which he had seen pictures. They lay there and kissed. It was the first time Ephriam felt up a girl. He liked feeling her breasts, but when Janice lifted her dress and pulled down her panties, he panicked. He jumped to his feet; now his heart was pumping wildly again! He didn't want to be a fourteen-year-old father! Janice was moving much too fast! "Ephriam, you can't put me in a family way if you just use your finger." He searched for excuses to avoid going any further. "What if somebody comes along and sees us? They'll tell my father." Janice was losing her patience. "Oh Ephriam, I thought you knew about what boys and girls do." Still standing and looking down at her, he dropped to his knees, and then lay next to her again. He was surprised when she got excited while he was feeling her with his finger, but then he remembered being told that girls "act that way" when a boy touches them "down there."

"Ephriam! Ephriam, where are you!" He jumped to his feet again. "That's my sister Anne. I got to go." Anne was calling from about fifty feet away and couldn't place exactly where Ephriam was. She called out, "Mother sent me to find you. Father wants us to go for a ride in Mr. Grime's new carriage."

He called out, "I'll be there shortly. Go back to the grove." He waited about a minute and then walked out from under the tree with Janice following just a couple of steps behind.

Curious, Anne decided to stay put. When Ephriam saw her he jumped back; he felt embarrassed. Anne had always looked up to him, her older brother. Now she would lose respect for him after discovering his sinning, especially with Janice Hull, a girl known to have a bad reputation.

That night he was lying in bed, exhausted from the busy picnic day. He was staring at the ceiling, feeling more regret for allowing his sister to discover his bad behavior.

Anne knocked lightly on his door. Not waiting for a response, she opened it slightly, whispering, "Will you rub my feet?" Ephriam sat up and nodded. Ever since Anne was three years old she had problems with her feet, and Ephriam would massage them. She sat on his bed and put her feet on his lap. The massage sessions had always served another purpose. They would talk, and over the years they would chat, gossip, and reveal harmless secrets, about people, places, and things. It was an uncommon example of brother and sister closeness. They both knew that as they got older the secrets they revealed to each other would become more complex, causing the re-setting of boundaries from time to time.

He spoke first. "I'm sorry you found me with Janice today." Anne had not planned to bring up the subject, but now felt she had to deal with it. "I can imagine what the two of you were doing under that tree. I guess I can understand why you would want to do it, but not with Janice Hull!" She almost forgot to talk quietly; awakening their parents would not be a good idea. "Ephriam, you can do a lot better than Janice Hull." He wanted to assure her that he had no plans to pursue a serious relationship with Janice, but he hesitated; wanting to be with a girl just for lustful purposes would only make him look worse. Rubbing the top and bottom of her feet and gently massaging her aching ankles, he simply said, "You are right, I'm going to stay away from her."

Anne said, "I would never tell anyone, mother, and certainly not father, what you were doing, you know that." He said, "I know you wouldn't, but I'm sorry you found out that I'm not the brother, or the man, you thought I was." Light from the moon shining in the window settled on her perfect smile. "I think you are just normal; you did what most curious boys try to do when it comes to girls. To me, you are still the best brother in the world."

Anne would always have a lot of influence over him. As summer passed she tried to get him interested in Catherine Witters again. She knew that during semester breaks and summer vacations while he attended Swatara Academy his resistance to Janice Hull's advances would be low. Catherine had changed; she had become curious about boys. She could keep Ephriam away from Janice and early fatherhood, which would result in him earning just enough to support her and their children.

Anne knew Ephriam, with Catherine, would have a picnic in the meadow, or sit on the Bernharter house's porch swing and talk about their futures, attend the spring dance, help with the children's Easter egg hunt, decorate the Christmas trees at each others' houses and at the church. Their friendship would be fulfilling, and perhaps someday they would marry after Ephriam completes his education.

Anne's plan seemed to be successful, at least for a while. For the remainder of that summer Ephriam and Catherine shared their time together.

One morning Sally mentioned she was going to the orphanage for visitation as a member of the ladies aid society. "Would you like to come along and visit with Johnny, the boy you met at the Sunday School picnic?" Ephriam hesitated because Johnny had told him the place was boring, but his desire to help less fortunate people influenced his decision. He decided to go.

When they arrived they noticed that Johnny was walking with crutches! He shouted Ephriam's name and started walking to him, shoving the crutches into the ground and dragging his feet along faster than he should have been. "I'm getting about much better!" Seeing him brought a smile to Ephriam's face; he had thought about him every time he'd run in a ball game, or play tag, or chase one of his classmates at school. He didn't think it was fair that he and other children were in perfect health, while some, like Johnny, had to suffer.

"I think you helped me at the picnic," Johnny declared. Ephriam laughed, recalling how he had enjoyed pushing

Johnny around in the wheelchair. "I can't believe I didn't overturn you, at least one time; I could have sent you rolling down the hill into the creek!"

Johnny wasn't laughing. "I'm not talking about the wheelchair; I'm talking about you touching me and getting that shock." Now Ephriam got serious too; he had tried to forget the incident. His fear of dying young disappeared when he was lying in the grass with Janice Hull. "I don't know what you're talking about, it was probably static electricity or something like that." Johnny stayed serious. "All I know is the day after that happened my legs started to tingle, and the next day I could move them a little. The next day they felt stronger, and here I am walking on crutches!" Ephriam said, "So what, that kind of stuff happens all the time. Don't tell anybody else about your silly notions, I don't need to have people making fun of me!"

Ephriam Bernharter and Johnny Erman became lifelong best friends. Johnny would eventually become John Erman. Regaining total use of his legs, he became a very successful attorney.

Chapter 4

1833

The time comes to enroll at Swatara Academy

It was time fourteen-year-old Ephriam to embark on the academic career that his father had so much wanted for him. It was the day Ephriam was to be enrolled at Swatara Academy for Boys. He would be away from home for the first time. He had dreaded its arrival. On the chilly fall Monday, very early in the morning, he and his father rode the buggy five miles West to the school in the town of Jenkinstown. The academy required all first year students to live in the residence hall. The headmaster and faculty wanted the opportunity to build character under the school's strict discipline. Learning skills that lead to a stable Christian lifestyle - cleaning his room, performing kitchen duty, adopting proper dining manners, proper grooming, and maintaining his wardrobe - are all part of the plan to make every boy attending the private school mature into a young man who would attend a university, learn and practice a profession, attain wealth, and become a leader of the community.

Ephriam knew he was going to have a difficult time adjusting to life at Swatara. He knew he was going to miss his mother, and he knew he would worry about Anne mostly because he wouldn't be able to shield her from jealous girls in school and from boys with bad intentions. He would miss Catherine; she promised him she would be faithful. He would miss his teacher Miss Noll. He would miss getting that firm handshake from his grandfather after church services. He would miss all the people who lived in Hamlin's neat, quaint houses; most people knew him all his life and called out to him by his first name when he passed them sitting on their porches or tending to their gardens. He felt secure and nurtured because all these people were interested in him; they would ask him if he was still doing good in school, if he was eating well, if he was getting all his chores done. Sally taught him to always acknowledge people when they greeted him. "If you are walking by their house, even if you are running or skipping, you stop and return their conversation, especially the old people; many of them don't have anybody to talk to until Sunday church." They'd talk to him in German. "Mother, Miss Noll told us in class we should speak English, not German, because English is what everyone in the big cities speak." Sally didn't want to contradict her children's teacher. "You answer a person in whichever language they are talking to you; that's being courteous. There are plenty of people in America who talk German."

He would even miss his father, who probably should have given his son more compliments, patting him on the shoulder occasionally, smiling at him more often, sharing conversation about history, sports, or hunting, instead of continuing his portrayal of a driven, stern father, setting the objectives and insisting on attainment.

Ephriam knew he had to accept without protest his father's high expectations; he would study hard because disappointing his family and friends was unimaginable to him. Ephriam had little to worry about though, for he was disciplined, more so than most young scholars; he was a near perfect student. More importantly, he wanted to eventually be successful; he was now reasonably sure he wanted to become a minister. He was confident he could adjust to the demanding regiments of the academy.

Religion class at Swatara inspired him, solidifying the faith his grandfather had instilled in him since he was old enough to understand about God. He and his classmates were reminded daily of the power of prayer, and the incident with Johnny kept re-entering his mind; he included him in his prayers each night. He kept wondering if his prayers could be more powerful than other people's. Most of the time he denied the possibility, though, he never mentioned his thoughts about it to anyone, especially his father, who wouldn't believe it, who never would be able to deal with his son being "different."

When he went home for a weekend, and during semester and summer breaks, he got to see Johnny, who always wanted to talk about his legs and the progress he was making regaining full use of them.

"The people at the orphanage think my cure is a miracle, but they don't know that you prayed for me. I never told them that." Ephriam told him the same thing he told him before. "Johnny, I didn't pray for you; I just touched you by accident for one second."

Jeremiah Rothermel was the strict headmaster of Swatara Academy. He was always affable and responsive to the parents of the academy's students. During admissions interviews, parent's weekends, or other events that brought the families of students to campus, he portrayed a sincere and friendly school administrator with a warm regard and genuine concern for the boys. However, the boys saw a different side. During typical times at the school he would go into tirades, yelling, screaming and swearing when forced to confront even the most trivial and minor rules infractions. He reminded all the students, especially the freshmen, that they were required to conform to the school's discipline and strict daily schedule, and to maintain excellent grades. If any student failed to meet the school's standards, they were expelled, sent home in disgrace. Students had long ago nicknamed him "Rotten Rothermel."

There was no relief from the stress imposed on freshmen. They arose every morning at 4:45 a.m. Physical training outdoors, regardless of the weather, was conducted until 5:30 a.m. Then housekeeping chores until breakfast at 6:15 a.m. At 6:45 a.m. students attended study hall until their first classes began at 8 a.m. Lunch was at 11:30 a.m. A full schedule of afternoon classes followed. After dinner at 5 p.m. evening study hall was held until lights out at 9 p.m. Assemblies, held occasionally with boring guest speakers, were a welcome break from the daily schedule.

Freshmen, supervised by seniors, cleaned their rooms, the hallways and other common areas, washed windows, and performed kitchen duties consisting of table serving, cleaning up, and washing dishes. Even dining was under strict rules. Each table had a senior in charge who made sure that the rules about passing of food, the placement of utensils and dinner ware, posture, and roll call, were all strictly followed. Headmaster Rothermel imposed stress relentlessly. Everyday there was more to study, more to remember, more to read and more to write, inflicted to build strong character while conditioning each young man to excel in academics and athletics.

Things were better for the sophomores; they were victims of slightly less intimidation by the seniors, and they took their meals under less strict protocol. Juniors were treated more kindly, although reminded by the seniors they were still inferior underclassmen.

The faculty was tough on every student; they were demanding and inflexible to all students regardless of class membership. Karl Sharman was Ephriam's favorite instructor because he was willing to spend extra time with the students, not only helping him with his academics, but encouraging him to set goals, and reminding him that he should go to seminary only if he felt he had a calling from God. "You must really want to be willing to commit your life to such a demanding career." Mr. Sharman's counseling convinced Ephriam there were faculty members at the academy that truly cared for the students.

Students were issued tablets and pencils needed due to do the large amount of writing required. Books were shared. Seniors eventually received some respect from the faculty during spring, four to six weeks before graduation, and after final exams.

It took a student the entire four years of hard work to earn Swatara Academy's acceptance as one of its own. It took many years before Ephriam was described by the school as a "distinguished graduate."

All schools, private or public, have traditions. People who work there, whether they're instructors, administrators, counselors, as well as cooks and janitors, make up the spirit and the character of an institution. Elmer Ganton was the school janitor for over twenty-five years; he was part of the soul of Swatara Academy. He was a gigantic man, 6'3", weighing over 325 pounds. He wore bib overalls, a T-shirt, and large boots. Always grouchy, he barked orders to the young men as if they were prison inmates. Elmer's job was to make sure the students did their cleaning properly.

On a day he was sent to the library to retrieve a book his teacher needed, Ephriam turned the hallway corner and came upon Elmer lying on the floor, on his left side – he had slipped and injured his hip. He was resisting crying out, but the expression on his face was a clear reaction to excruciating pain. Just as Ephriam got to him he regained his composure, but after making a quick attempt, realized he was unable to get to his feet. Instead of having to endure the embarrassment resulting from a loud shout for help, he barked at Ephriam, "Go get some people to help me get up." Instead, Ephriam knelt down and asked, "Are you in pain? Where does it hurt?" Elmer had no patience with the boy. "Do as I say. Go get some help, or I'll have you whipped!" Ignoring the man's demands, Ephriam put one hand on his hip and extended his other hand to the big old man and started to pull him up. Feeling his heart beating rapidly and skipping beats, he was gasping for breath. He kept his hand on Elmer's hip and allowed the horrible pain to diminish and the fracture to mend. Logic said it couldn't happen, but Elmer Ganton got to his feet. He began limping down the hall toward the office; stopping and turning back to look in amazement at the young boy that just performed an impossible task.

Ephriam got no thanks from Elmer Ganton. He refused to believe what had happened. Ganton's doctor told him that he had never seen a hip that severely bruised without being broken.

Ephriam was just as surprised as Ganton at what happened. He had intended to comply with the man's loud demands to go for help, but he suddenly suspected he could do a lot more. Getting the big man on his feet by touching him, plus Johnny Erman starting to walk, made it difficult to deny that he had something to do with it. He would accept he had special powers only after seeking advice from someone he felt he could confide in. He certainly didn't want the intolerance of Headmaster Rothermel, the faculty, fellow students, and more importantly his father, to cause him to be expelled from Swatara Academy. For now he felt his secret was safe because he doubted Elmer Ganton would tell anybody that a young student helped him. Probably nobody would believe him even if he did.

A few days later, desperate, he went to see Mr. Sharman. He described what happened with Elmer Ganton. He told him about Johnny Erman

"Ephriam, if you are asking me if it's possible you have special powers, my answer is yes." Ephriam was surprised to hear that. "I'm a Christian, so I believe that Jesus healed the sick. Despite many in the church preaching that only Jesus had that power, I believe that men with intense faith can also heal." Ephriam said, "But I don't think I have intense faith. I believe in God, but so does almost everyone else." Sharman responded, "Perhaps your faith is stronger than you realize. Ephriam wasn't getting the answers he wanted to hear. "I don't want any special powers. I don't want to be looked at as some freak." Sharman said, "Pray to God for guidance. You don't need to tell anyone you can heal people. Keep it to yourself, eventually God will tell you what to do with your gift." It was advice that Ephriam intended to heed. Meanwhile, until he received some kind of message, he would attempt to live with his situation.

He had not been sleeping very well since Elmer Ganton's fall. After seeing Mr. Sharman, he felt better. He went to bed early and quickly fell asleep. His deep slumber was short-lived. He was awakened by a voice growling his name. Startled, he sat up, rubbed his eyes, and tried to focus on who was sitting in front of him on the windowsill. "Ephriam! You mustn't sleep while I'm visiting! You need to be a good host and listen to the message I have brought you!" He glanced over at his roommates and was surprised they were still sleeping. "Who are you? How did you get in here?" He couldn't see the man's face, for the room was dark; the only light was from the moon shining on his back, creating a silhouette. He responded with a growl, slow and deliberate. "Who I am is not important, but my message for you is." Ephriam ruled out that he was dreaming; he pinched his arm and it hurt. Suddenly the dark stranger leaped to the ceiling, landing on his feet and walking across it until he was hanging like a bat over Ephriam's head. Now the slow, deep growl seemed to have an eerie echo effect. "I've been told you have special powers, but I bet you can't walk on ceilings." Ephriam jumped up and grabbed at the creatures hanging arms, hoping to pull this odd being down on the bed. When he touched his hands they began glowing, turning a bright orange, moving slowly up to his chest, then up to his legs, like a stove pipe being gradually illuminated by the increasing intensity of burning embers. Finally his head began to glow, but then, like a chameleon, he became dark again. Ephriam lit the lamp on his nightstand and saw that the creature was dwarf-like with red bristled hair, ashen scaly skin and pink eyes with blood red pupils; a pale blue smoke was emanating from his ears, his nose, and the corners of his mouth. "I have been sent to warn you; abandon this notion that you can be like Jesus Christ and make sick people well!" Ephriam, frightened, somehow found the courage to ask again, "Who are you? Where are you from?" He got a quick, growling response. "Don't you know an angel when you see one?" Ephriam's reply was confrontational. "You are no angel. Angels are beautiful; you are repulsive." That made him laugh. "If I was beautiful you wouldn't take me seriously. Some angels are beautiful, some aren't." Ephriam asked, "Do you have a name?" Suddenly the creature got serious and appeared anxious to leave. "Know me as a miscreant, but call me Daytrin; I only need a name when I must live among your kind." Then he began his sermon; "I have been sent to curse you, to mark you, so the evil force will always know where you are! Heed my warning! If you use your powers to heal the sick and infirm you will live a life filled with tragedy and regret, for my curses are terrible curses."

Ephriam saw and heard all he needed to be convinced he was having an encounter with a demon. He had learned early in life while listening to his grandfather that demons are generally considered to be angels who have fallen from grace by rebelling against God. He watched the despicable creature, still upside down, expose and then fondle his penis, similar to the drawings of jungle primates masturbating that Ephriam had seen depicted in anthropologic textbooks. His member began growing; it achieved an incredible length while staying flaccid; and soon it was long enough to hang down and extend to his shoulder! He began spraying Ephriam, his bed sheets, and his mattress with urine; then the spray became a steady, heavy stream of dark yellow liquid that filled the room with such a putrid and foul smell it caused Ephriam to be sick. Suddenly, in an instant, the demon ran across the ceiling and jumped out the window, vanishing into thin air.

Everyone was asleep; the clock showed 1:17 a.m. Ephriam stripped the sheets from his bed and dragged the mattress down the hallway very quietly to the laundry and supply room. He was aware the code of conduct forced any student encountering him to report the incident to the tyrant Rothermel, who would accuse him of bed-wetting, violating curfew, and destroying school property, and then expel him. He washed the sheets in a laundry tub and found clean bedding and an extra mattress. Before he could drag the new mattress to his room he needed to dispose of the polluted one. He slowly opened the large, heavy oak door and dragged the horrible smelling thing about 50' into the woods. Then, while sneaking back into the dormitory, he was startled once again. Noticing a bright light suddenly reflecting in the door glass, he turned and looked into the woods and saw the mattress ablaze, being burned up by a furious fire, with its flames shooting high into the sky! Remarkably, all of these late night exploits went undetected. He was curious why the demon cursed him. Was it because Satan didn't want yet another healer demonstrating God's power?

He still considered his power to help sick and infirmed people a liability; he intended to keep it a secret. He wanted to become a normal pastor and teach his parishioners their prayers will be answered if they have strong faith, and not to depend on him to touch them and pray for their healing. He didn't want that responsibility, raising false hopes, failing and causing pain, grief and disappointment.

Chapter 5

1834

Going to Harrisburg, and Anne disappears

The summer before Ephriam entered his sophomore year at Swatara Academy, Henry and Sally Bernharter, along with Ephriam and fourteen-year-old Anne took the train to Harrisburg to attend an agricultural exposition and to visit relatives who lived in the capital city.

Anne had become moody and confrontational, behavior that is expected from a teenage girl going through the physical and emotional changes that occur while maturing. Despite her ill-behaved temperament, Ephriam and Anne had remained close. Anne was a beautiful girl. She looked much older than her fourteen years. Men found her beauty breathtaking. Her blonde, almost white hair, her near perfect facial features, blue eyes and sensuous lips, along with her slender build, always attracted attention from the boys.

Enthralled by the big city and dreaming of becoming an actress, she asked to accompany the adults to the theater. When Henry told her she was too young to attend, she launched into one of her moody tantrums. He spoke firmly, "You must learn you cannot have everything you want!" Her foot stomping and glares continued while he and Sally, excited about spending the long planned evening with friends, dressed for dinner and the theater.

After Anne appeared to regain her composure, Ephriam made an offer. "I'll take you downstairs to the hotel's tea room. We can have something to eat and drink, talk, and pretend we're socialites." Anne's disposition quickly turned positive. "I can be a debutante, the daughter of a wealthy German prince who is visiting with the governor!" Ephriam laughed. "Anne, you have such an astonishing imagination, I don't know if mother and father will ever be able to understand you. You want to live faster than any person I know."

She wasn't paying much attention to what he was saying; she was excitingly searching through the closet perusing her mother's wardrobe, selecting clothing that she could wear that would costume the role she was about to play.

They were escorted to a delightful table at the window, giving them the added joy of watching fashionable people, out for the evening, pass by, the dashing young men with their slicked back hair and stiff high collars and their chic, bejeweled ladies with their large and fancy plumed hats and elegant long dresses. Broad smiles and loud laughter reigned as they strolled the wooden walkways to the city's busy, brightly lit restaurants and theaters.

Anne gave her performance while Ephriam watched with amusement. Her costume and make-up made her appear to be eighteen years old, and Ephriam, wearing his Sunday gray wool suit, easily passed as her twenty-one-year-old escort. It was the first time he looked at her and realized she was never again going to be that little girl he once knew. He noticed the men staring at her when they were being seated. He relished their envy, sure they were thinking how fortunate he was to be escorting such a lovely young lady. Looking across the table at her, he was sure if she weren't his sister he would pur-

sue her romantically; he would make love to her, smell her
sweet fragrance, feel her, and taste her for hours and hours!
How so very un-natural thoughts, but how so very true!

They sampled strange foods, drank a variety of teas, and
finally indulged in luxurious desserts. Money was no problem; they charged everything to their parents' room!

They were enjoying their night out; they decided to worry about explaining the charges to their father later. They
began poking fun at some of the stranger people passing by.
Big noses, fat rear-ends, tall and skinny men and women,
short and plump men and women were all subjected to their
humorous scrutiny.

Anne, feeling a little light-headed from all the excitement, said, "I'm going outside to get some fresh air." Ephriam
hadn't eaten all of his dessert, so he stayed at their table. After a half-hour passed he went outside for her but didn't see
her. Thinking she might have returned to the room, he raced
up the stairs. She wasn't there; he was beginning to worry.
Outside again, he shouted her name, getting passersby's attention. One gentleman asked, "Who is missing?" Ephriam was
almost too panicky to acknowledge his question. "My sister.
She came out of the hotel to get some air, and now I don't see
her." Two women, overhearing the conversation, approached
him. "How old is the girl; what does she look like?" Ephriam
was pacing back and forth, thoughts of his parents reaction
filled his head. He would be punished for letting the girl out
of his sight, and Anne's punishment for running away would
be harsh. "She's fifteen years old, her blonde hair is pinned
up, and she's wearing an evening dress." It would have helped
if he had explained that the dress was a silk, light blue gown
not usually worn by such a young girl. He didn't know if she
decided to run away or if she was kidnapped. A policeman
walked up and asked, "How long has this lassie been missing?" Ephriam felt a little relieved when he saw the officer.
"She's been out of my sight for about an hour now." The po-

liceman laughed, "Oh, young man, that's nothing! I suspect you are a little jealous that she wants to see the town without you, heh?" Ephriam was not amused. "She's my sister! Whatever is causing her to be missing could have dangerous implications!" The policeman, walking away, turned and said, "I'll keep an eye out for the little thing." Ephriam didn't have any faith in the officer's efforts but shouted out to him nevertheless; "My family's name is Bernharter, we're staying at the Landon Hotel!"

He began walking the streets near the hotel looking for her. Another passerby had suggested he walk down to the park along the riverbank. "Perhaps she decided to take a walk along the Susquehanna." Ephriam searched the park for more than two hours. Then he hurried back to the hotel and wrote a note to his parents filled with lies designed to buy him more time to find her. He wrote that he had taken Anne downstairs to the restaurant to further calm her, when quite by accident he found one of his professors from Swatara Academy dining. The professor insisted that Ephriam and Anne join him for an evening at his home. He emphasized that they would be late coming back to the hotel, they should not stay up, and that Anne was feeling much better. He knew that he would be disciplined for taking Anne anywhere without getting their permission first, but at least Anne would not be punished.

After leaving the note, still terrified, he returned to the streets to resume his search. She was naive, not sophisticated enough to be wary of robbers, rapists and murderers that could be encountered in a large city. She had no money with her, but she was wearing one of their mother's valuable necklaces. Ephriam searched for hours. He looked at his pocket watch. It was 11 p.m; he knew his parents were by now hysterical. If he went back to the hotel without his sister they would accuse him of negligence for allowing her to be out of his sight, and if something would happen to her, they would remind him everyday for the rest of his life.

For now, however, he didn't have any time to worry about those things. He needed to concentrate on finding Anne before she is robbed, assaulted, raped, or murdered!

At about 2 a.m, so exhausted that he felt he couldn't go on anymore, he found her. Calling his name, she came running out of the darkness, across the moonlit meadow in the park. "Ephriam, guess what? I'm going to be married!" As they embraced, an old man walked slowly toward them. He was dressed in black, encased in a black cape with a red lining, and a black top hat. "Ephriam, this is Balair, I am going to be his wife!" Ephriam was stunned and speechless. The man was at least fifty years old; he had a beaked nose, black rotten teeth, and smelled of urine and sweat. Ephriam prepared to attack but then noticed that the man's feet were about twelve inches off the ground and that his whole body was beginning to turn a glowing red, his black outfit hiding it all except his head and hands. He wasn't a man at all, and when he saw Ephriam take notice, he snapped his fingers in front of Anne, causing her to become rigid, unable to move, even to blink her eyes.

His voice and mannerism, along with his apparel, mimicked that of a Shakespearian thespian. Ephriam watched the freak's eyes become pink while his pupils turned blood red while noticing that same pale blue smoke coming from his ears, nose and mouth, just as it did from Daytrin's. "You are responsible for bringing all of this about because you didn't take Daytrin's visit seriously." Ephriam looked at Anne, searching for a reaction from her. "Don't worry, she can't see or hear you. She is possessed; I will control her from now on. I will not abuse her as long as you cooperate with me. I now have the power to send her off to do terrible things. I think she will make a very efficient murderer, especially after I remove any sense of fear from her.

Ephriam felt powerless to do anything but listen and try to get answers to his questions. "When I need a young and beautiful girl to tempt a man, Anne will be quite right for the job." Ephriam was sickened by the talk while the creature continued. "And when I must give rewards for deeds done for me, all the fruit of Anne's young body will satisfy any man's appetite."

Ephriam was trying his best to ignore the hideous creature's profane discourse. Unabashed, he asked, "Have you done her any physical harm?" Balair began laughing. "You want to know if I fucked her don't you?" Ephriam, dreading to hear the answer, ignored the question. Balair revealed what took place.

"I approached Anne in front of the hotel, took her by the hand, and walked her to a peaceful spot along the water." Ephriam interrupted, "She didn't offer any resistance?" Balair laughed again. "Anne is human, and all humans are sinners. Since sinners can't resist evil, she couldn't resist taking my hand and going with me because I am an agent of Satan. I am a demon. You've learned that haven't you? Because she is the most cherished person in your life I have put some of Satan's evil spirit inside her; she is possessed. I control her now. If you continue to heal people I will destroy her!"

Ephriam snapped back. "If Satan needs to control me, why not possess me? What have I done to cause the wrath of Satan?" Balair explained, "Satan can't possess you because your soul is already possessed; it's possessed by the Holy Spirit. You are without the original sin that men are born with. When you use your power to heal through faith you are glorifying God, drawing attention to his goodness. That's why you must be watched." Ephriam was sure Balair used this honest explanation of things to convince him his threats were to be taken very seriously.

"She will do anything to anyone I command her to do. If you obey us Anne will live a normal life. If you disobey us I will make her do horrible and despicable acts. When I'm finished using her I will destroy her. I know you are an invocator." Ephriam wanted to know what invocators are. The demon, suddenly losing patience in answering questions, retorted, "You'll know when you need to know, if you ever need to know, and not one minute sooner!"

Anne remained rigid and erect, like a statue of a beautiful Greek Goddess. Balair detailed in his deep, resonant voice, what happened when he and Anne were alone. "Part of Satan's spirit is in my breath; I exhaled it into her. I kissed her lips and exhaled it into her mouth, sending it deep into her lungs. I also blew into her ears and nostrils. Then she lifted her dress and pulled down her panties, graciously spreading her legs while I blew the vapor into her maiden vessel; that particular part you would have loved to perform!" Ephriam was so outraged he couldn't find the words for a response. He finally blurted, "I'll kill you for doing this to her!" Balair laughed and then responded like an actor reciting from Hamlet, "You fool, you can't kill me; I'm not mortal! I've been dead for 934 years!" Then he waved his hand toward Anne; her ears, her nose, and her lips started giving off that pale blue haze. "Satan is in her, she is possessed, let this be your warning; don't disobey me! Heal the sick or the infirm, and I will destroy her. I will explode her heart, I will bring about a massive stroke. I will have her murdered. I will have her raped. I will have her drowned. I will have her fall from a cliff. I will butcher her alive and devour her. I will set her afire. I will have the bull gore her. I will have a horse trample her to death. I will make her blue eyes turn black and be sightless. I will cripple her arms. I will cripple her legs." Ephriam was shocked into total silence; no response from him was possible. Balair walked behind him, and when Ephriam turned around he was gone.

Anne awakened; she walked over to him and fell into his arms; he held and comforted her. "Ephriam, I'm so tired. I had only wanted to take a short walk; I got lost and I don't remember where I went. I'm sorry; I know I caused you to worry. Please don't tell father." While they walked back to the hotel he told her about the note he had written to their parents. "They will be quite angry with me for keeping you out late, but the anger will be directed toward me. The resulting punishment given to me will be less severe than what you would face if father was told his daughter ran away from home."

When they got back to the hotel there was a note at the desk for them, brought by a messenger from Henry telling Ephriam that the husband of one of the couples they were attending the theatre with had become seriously ill and was taken to the doctor. They had been asked to stay with his wife until he was stabilized. It wasn't until after 6 a.m. that Henry and Sally returned to their hotel room. They never knew about Ephriam and Anne's harrowing evening when their daughter got lost. Neither did they know, nor did Anne herself know, that on that evening her soul became possessed by Satan.

Two days later the family visited one of Henry's cousins, Sam Michaels and his wife June. Sam was a former coal miner from the northern part of Schuylkill County. He had developed a serious lung condition, a result of breathing coal dust during the many years he worked in the damp, black underground. June told Henry and Sally, "He suffers so much it breaks my heart; he's always out of breath; he has seizures and his coughing causes him much pain."

Sam was confined to a chair in the living room, too sick to come to the dinner table or to even get into bed. He slept in the chair most nights. June explained, "Just trying to walk to the next room causes him to be completely out of breath, and then he coughs and gasps for air until he falls down and passes out." Sam did his best to carry on a conversation with his guests, but he hardly had enough breath to speak.

Witnessing the awful suffering Sam Michaels was forced

to endure overwhelmed Ephriam. Ephriam couldn't bring himself to blame the coalminer if he lost his faith in God. He knew he had to try and give the man his life back and to restore joy to his family.

When it was time for the Bernharters to leave, Ephriam excused himself while everyone was walking to the carriage. "I forgot my scarf." When he went back into the house he noticed Sam Michaels was sleeping, opening his eyes every few seconds; he no longer could sleep soundly. When Ephriam walked over to him he became startled; with the look of fear on his face he fought to get out of his chair, but it was a hopeless effort. He was gasping for breath as Ephriam laid his hand on his forehead. "Please don't hurt me, please. I'm begging you!" Ephriam whispered, "In the name of the Father, the Son, and the Holy Ghost, Amen." Sam Michaels' body became limp; he wasn't fighting any longer. Ephriam looked down and saw the man's deep-set eyes affixed on him, a helpless, penetrating and hollow haunting stare. Ephriam's heart started skipping beats; he felt the sensation as the air was sucked out of his lungs. He was having the same sensations; he was scared but not as much as before.

Sam Michaels kept staring, his eyes following Ephriam as he moved toward the door. Ephriam held his finger to his lips and whispered, "What I just did is between you and me; you need to pray to God; you can be healed." Daytrin and Balair must never know what he did for Sam Michaels.

About a month later Michaels' coughing was becoming less frequent and not as severe. He began to breathe more easily; six months later he was walking about.

Chapter 6

1837

The summer after graduating from Swatara Academy

For Ephriam, graduating from Swatara Academy was like being released from prison. He savored the freedom.

He was anxious to have the time off. He knew the summer of 1837 would be short; before long he would be leaving for seminary in Philadelphia. He knew being enrolled there would mean long hours of study, but he was anxious to get started.

He was also anxious to spend time with Catherine. They started taking long walks and doing more than just kissing. Catherine was cooperative; they would take blankets to a secluded spot, get undressed and engage in heavy petting. Eventually the inevitable happened; they engaged in sexual intercourse. Fortunately they came to their senses; they knew they were putting Ephriam's entire future in jeopardy. Occasionally they would have sex, but they didn't carry it to orgasm. They hoped that this would minimize the risk of Catherine getting pregnant and complicating their lives and those of their families.

They spent long hours sitting on the porch swing at her

house talking about the future. On one of those hot summer days while they enjoyed glasses of cold lemonade, Catherine stated, "Ephriam, our classmates at school always talked about you doing some kind of ritual on Johnny Erman, and then he started to walk." She had wanted to question him before but never had the courage to ask. Even though they weren't courting, and they weren't engaged, they were having a serious relationship, so it was important to her now to know the details. "Did you pray for him? Do you think you got God to make him walk?" Ephriam couldn't deny to himself any longer that he had special powers, but now he had demons to worry about; they could kill Anne. He knew it was important to prevent Catherine from spreading gossip about him. "I just said a prayer for Johnny, after all, I am going to be a minister, I may as well practice!" They both laughed; she reacted with relief, and when he noticed that her curiosity seemed to be satisfied, he felt with some assurance that she wouldn't gossip that he was a "faith healer." Anyone doing that would not please the demons.

Chapter 7

1837

Ephriam becomes closer to his sister – Anne

The ever wise and observant Anne watched as Ephriam and Catherine became love struck. She knew her brother, a healthy young man, would probably give up all his ambitions for the ministry if he could be married to Catherine. Sex had such intense power! She used the opportunity to talk with him when they sat on the front porch step one hot summer night. She held his right hand up to her cheek, and then gave it a gentle kiss. "Be careful Ephriam, accidents do happen, and there isn't room in your life for fatherhood." He countered, "I have no intention of becoming a father!" Anne wanted to be helpful, not confrontational. "I know you and Catherine are having sex, and that means you could get her in trouble." Shaking his head, he said, "Why do I have to be blessed with a nosy baby sister!" She quickly responded, "I'm just watching out for you because I love you. Just be careful."

That summer was a time of reflection for the brother and his sister; they spent a lot of time together. "Remember when I took that walk when we were in Harrisburg and I got lost?" He nodded, reluctant to talk at length about that scary evening. "Of course I remember, how could I forget something like that?" He was expecting her to ask him again for forgiveness. "It was like I lost consciousness; I don't know where I went; I don't remember any of it. I don't know what happened to me during that brief time." He was troubled by the look of despair on her face. "Sometimes I feel so vulnerable."

He was the only mortal to know what really happened to her during those hours she was lost, but he could never tell her. He discouraged her from dwelling on the experience. "Maybe you are worrying too much about it. Everything turned out satisfactory. Just treat it as a bad memory, a life lesson." The frustrated look on her face bothered him, but he was just thankful she wouldn't ever remember her ordeal.

Ephriam and Anne definitely did not want their parents to overhear these conversations. If Henry found out that his daughter had spent hours wandering the streets of Harrisburg, he would send her off to a boarding school – an institution for girls that would ensure that she get an education and find her place in society.

It was about this time that Catherine decided to end her relationship with Ephriam. Ephriam was relieved. They both came to realize there wasn't going to be enough time for them to sustain their relationship while he attended seminary. She wasn't sure she could make the commitment that would be necessary to be the wife of a minister. She wished for a life less complicated. She eventually married a cabinetmaker and gave birth to three daughters.

Chapter 8

1837

Ephriam leaves for Seminary in Philadelphia

Ephriam left for seminary in August 1837. He had never imagined a city the size of Philadelphia. Hotels, restaurants, shops and offices all lit up. He marveled at the elegant carriages, chauffeured by neatly uniformed teamsters and pulled by sleek, ornately plumed horses with shiny black tack. He had never seen so many people gathered together before. They strolled, some hurried, up and down the walkways. There were an endless number of taverns; men smoked their cigars while discussing business and politics. The women shopped the millinery stores, patronized the dressmakers, and had tea at sidewalk cafes.

On Sunday mornings the cathedrals, churches, chapels, and meeting halls were full of worshippers. Early on Ephriam took up the habit of taking long walks Sunday mornings to listen to the church choirs sing the complex anthems and the all to familiar common hymns sung in the country churches like St. Luke's.

He listened to the sermons; the conservative voices of the parish priests, the fire and brimstone message bursting from the sanctuary of the Baptist church. The Lutheran ministers gave their message of salvation through grace. Reverend Bernharter, known simply as Luther to his peers, had occasionally in years past traveled to Philadelphia for seminars. Whenever he visited the city he was invited to preach at one of the churches. Ephriam's family pride was enriched knowing his grandfather could hold his own in the big city's pulpits. He would tell Ephriam how he would make sure his visiting sermons were pointed. "They didn't feel too comfortable while I scolded, prodded, challenged, and demanded redemption from them; I'd put a burr under the asses of those wealthy, finely dressed sinners sitting there in their fancy churches!" Then he would roar with laughter. Ephriam would go home and tell his mother that grandpa used a bad word. Sally would bend down and tell her son, "Whisper in my ear the bad word grandpa used." Reluctantly Ephriam would whisper "ass." Sally quickly straightened up and called out "Henry!" Henry, holding his newspaper, came into the room from the parlor, prepared to deal with a crisis. "Henry, your father is using profanity around our boy again; he doesn't need to hear the word 'ass' coming from his minister grandfather's lips, you need to talk to him once again." Henry told him, "Don't say ass, say behind," and then went back into the parlor. Sally yelled, "I didn't mean you need to talk to Ephriam, he already knows not to use those kind of words. I meant you need to talk to your minister father!"

The Lutheran Theological Seminary was a vast place, and for a newcomer like Ephriam it was naturally difficult to navigate the many buildings, long corridors, and endless number of classrooms. He was immediately hurled into a rigorous schedule: attending daily church, prayers, research, writing, speaking, Bible studies, religion instruction, and all the other required classes.

After being at seminary for only a few weeks, he met perhaps the most influential person who ever entered his life,

Reverend Frank Herr. A long friendship began when Herr became Ephriam's mentor and religious theory professor. Herr was a short, impish, bow-legged man with close-cropped gray hair. He spoke with a high pitched dignified German accent. Wherever he was, there was the aroma of sweet cherry tobacco coming from his curved pipe that was always in his mouth. In his cluttered office, its walls covered with bookshelves, and hundreds of books and papers lying on the floor, he would sit back in his overstuffed brown leather desk chair and slowly puff on his pipe while contemplating an answer to an involved question.

Ephriam was accustomed to teachers pointing their fingers and challenging, "How can you study for the ministry when you doubt the Bible, the word of God? " Herr could be talked to without accusing the young student of questioned faith. Reverend Herr became Ephriam's closest friend because he attempted to satisfy the young man's doubts about God and Christianity.

Ephriam's questioning his own faith was his way of establishing and expanding his beliefs. Herr understood and encouraged that approach. He was the only professor that did so.

Ephriam wanted to ask the wise old man if he believed some people had the power to heal others, but he didn't dare. Being asked such a question would put Herr in the precarious position of knowing a student believed he experienced a phenomenon that was contrary to the church's teaching. Ephriam knew a freshman student who became mixed up in controversy involving church doctrine is soon shown to the door, and he could harm Herr's credibility and reputation. He decided his course of action would be silence.

Frank Herr had taught long enough to know Ephriam was a special student. His ability to evaluate students quickly wasn't just the result of experience; he used intuition. Ephriam's discipline as a scholar impressed him quite a bit; the young man excelled because of Miss Noll's teaching, Luther Bernharter's hard disciplined study sessions, and the constant reminder of Henry Bernharter's high expectations.

Seminary students learned early they couldn't put anything over on Professor Herr. He would state in class, especially to the new, incoming students, "You may think you are smarter than I am, but let me tell you, I already know which of you are going to preach the Lord's Word to a congregation, and which of you are going to clerk in a store!"

He encouraged Ephriam to study the piano in order to complement the vocal music training that was part of the curriculum. Ephriam eventually learned to play well enough to accompany choral groups in hymn sings and to play some of the classical pieces of the great composers.

Chapter 9

1838

Ephriam meets Jeanie Belvoir

On a rare afternoon off, he was having a cup of coffee and reading some lighthearted fare at one of the local cafes near campus. A young black girl wearing an old worn out gray coat and a maroon stocking cap pulled down over her ears, just barely clearing her eyes, tapped on the window to get his attention. She motioned for him to come outside. It was cold, and she wanted him to get her a cup of coffee. "Here's the money, you're a student ain't you? They don't let coloreds in there you know, nor use the china cups." Ephriam said, "I'll pay for your coffee." He brought out coffee in a small carafe and poured it into the old tin cup she held in her shaking bare hands. Light rain began to freeze as she sipped the coffee in the frigid cold. They moved under a building's overhang; he stayed with her.

He had never met a person like her. She was skinny and short, 4' 10" tall, weighed about ninety pounds, short nappy hair and beautiful light brown skin. Her facial features were blended and near perfect. Ephriam was awestruck by her beauty; it was obvious to him she was the offspring of an interracial relationship. She told him her name was Jeanie Belvoir, and she was a slave girl.

Ice in her hair and on her eyebrows, she was shivering all over now, still holding the hot cup of coffee in both hands, her fingers wrapped tightly around the heated cup. He noticed how thin and ragged the coat was. "I was born and grew up in Louisiana, that's why I have this French accent. I'll never get used to cold weather." He had noticed the accent right away. He was enjoying listening to her. "Later my master sent me to Tennessee. He hired me out to a man and his wife who had thirteen children, and a mess of cousins, nephews, nieces, plus grandparents and aunts and uncles!"

When her master's daughter married the son of a wealthy Philadelphia shipping magnate, she was brought to Philadelphia to work seven days a week from sunrise to sunset as a housekeeper. "I could have my freedom, Pennsylvania is a free state. I could also travel to Canada; they can't send anybody up there to bring me back. But I stay because I don't know nobody in Canada or anywhere else." He said, "There are plenty of abolitionists that would find people to help you in Canada." She said, "I don't want to live in Canada; its colder there than here, and I'd probably just end up doing the same job I do here." Ephriam found her life's story fascinating; he had read about slavery, but he never gave serious thought to the plight of Negroes. Occasionally an escaped slave would wander into the mountains near Hamlin. They would build crude huts and live off the land while hiding. When the bounty hunters came the locals wouldn't cooperate, choosing to allow the poor souls to live in chronic poverty; that was the price they paid for their freedom. Ephriam said, "But you'd be paid. You'd have money and could quit and find another job if you wanted to." He could see she didn't want to discuss it anymore. He concluded she was reasonably happy with her life and evidently had some freedoms or she wouldn't be allowed to be out about.

Ephriam felt comfortable being with her, for she was friendly and seemed very intelligent. He told her to meet him the next evening in the vestibule of old main hall; he would bring her a cup of hot coffee and a piece of cake or pie. Despite rules against non-students being in main hall, nobody seemed to take note of them sitting on the floor over in a corner near the door. They began meeting there most evenings when Ephriam didn't have late classes. They talked for hours at a time; they became good friends despite their cultural and racial differences. Ephriam especially liked her because she always said what she thought, never holding anything back. They talked about religion, politics, history, the classics; Ephriam was amazed how a girl with such a disadvantaged life could be so brilliant, informed, and cultured as she was. "My master's daughter Miss Susan taught me to read, even though she was told not to. She gave me books; I'd light a candle and read late into the night." Slaves that could read were always considered a threat. "He would have beaten me and taken me to the auction if he found out I could read."

Now Ephriam was hearing about slavery first hand. He had grown up in a society that was very proper; you kept many of your views to yourself. Talking about radical political ideas, or exploring different philosophies, was taboo in Hamlin. He told her, "In my home town we aren't prejudice; we believe all men are equal, we're all children of God." Jeanie laughed when she heard that. "You come from a town where the people have been closed off for years from the real world; they never saw Negroes or Chinamen. It's easy not to hate them when you never see them." He had to admit she was right.

Ephriam was anxious to broaden his horizons. After all, it was all part of his education: meeting different people, experiencing other cultures, sampling their food and customs, appreciating the way they dress, the churches they attended, the languages and dialects they spoke, and the accents that added flavor to their English. He was certain his grandfather had similar experiences when he attended this same seminary in this same, glorious, exciting city. He felt sorry for his father, an intelligent man who missed his social discourse when he chose the blacksmith trade over ordination.

This interracial friendship would not be possible back home, but the two of them, a tall and sturdy young man of German ancestry, and a skinny little black girl with nappy hair seen together sitting on the floor reading in the main hall's vestibule, or walking down the street indulging in animated conversation, or sitting on a park bench feeding the squirrels and pigeons, was lost among the mass of big city busyness. Practically nobody noticed them; maybe it was because nobody could imagine romance with such an odd coupling.

Ephriam spent most daylight hours attending class or in the library doing research. Evenings were spent in his room writing reports and preparing for the next day's classes. Later in the night he would meet Jeanie. They would share a cup of coffee in the dark corner of the vestibule. Eager to experiment with ideas borne from the Age of Enlightenment, Ephriam was delighted to have a friend who was so very different from him. It was typical of campus life; she would listen while he would elucidate his inner thoughts about life. Jeanie was willing to listen to everything his imagination managed to put into words. Sometimes they talked until 2 a.m.

She still wore the ragged coat, jerking the maroon stocking cap off her head when they slid into their dark corner. He wanted to see under the long tattered gray coat, but she only allowed occasional glimpses. The tattered dress was sheer and cut very short. He was surprised when the coat fell away when she pulled her knees up to rest her chin on her arms; she wasn't wearing any panties!

Ephriam was living with less sleep and more coffee, but his conversations with Jeanie were so inspiring he felt losing sleep to find more inner perspective was a good trade-off.

†

Chapter 10

1839

Ephriam confesses. Jeanie discloses her special mission

Ephriam and Jeanie had to be discreet. Even though their relationship had been platonic, gossips could make trouble for a young divinity student spending time alone with any girl, and a scandal would surely result if some scuttlebutt played it up that the girl is a Negro. If he were called into his dean's office to explain a relationship that had the potential to embarrass the school, his grandfather, his family, and also Jeanie's owners, his continued enrollment at the school would be seriously jeopardized.

Despite the risk, he couldn't stay away from her. He contemplated for weeks telling her about his ability to heal; he wanted so badly to share his dilemma with a friend, and she was his best friend. He was sure she would offer better advice than Mr. Sharman; eventually God will give divine instruction how to use the gift.

One day she suggested he meet her at the door to the rescue mission a few blocks from campus where he and some of his classmates did volunteer work occasionally. She needed him to get her in; there they could be warm and have some free soup.

Deciding to use this opportunity, he blurted, "I think I can heal people. I touch the sick or infirm, and they get better." Jeanie reacted without the surprise he expected. He continued, "When it happens my heart starts racing and I lose my breath. It feels like all the air is sucked out of my lungs. I get scared every time it happens." He felt relieved that he finally confessed to her.

"Ephriam, I've known all along that you got healing powers!" He could hardly believe his ears. "You of all people, a student of the Bible, should see that God's picked you to be special." She was displaying still more of her wisdom he had come to respect. "Don't you know why we've been able to talk so good? It's because special powers are at work here, forces beyond you have thrown us together."

"Who or what are these forces with special powers, and how come you know so much about all of this?" As a divinity student he was very familiar with the conflicts going on among heavenly forces that are described in the Bible. Jeanie said, "If you can heal, then you must have been chosen by God to be an invocator." He snapped. "I've heard that term before. I don't know what being an invocator means." Jeanie stayed patient while he got more agitated as a result of her suggestion. Then she confessed, "I just follow my orders. Invocators are mortals who carry out God's orders." Just following orders? He wondered what that meant.

He said, "I don't want to be an invocator; where does it say anything in the Bible about invocators?" She spoke up, "Invocator is Satan's name for it; it ain't in the Bible. You're studying to be a minister, don't be so Goddamned stupid!" He was surprised to hear her talk that way. Surprise turned to terror when she declared, "You're going to be spending the rest of your life with me whether you like it or not. Satan has ordered me to stop you from ever using your heal-

ing powers; you've already been cursed, and you've already
been warned." He stood up and headed for the mission's
chapel. She followed him while he hollered; "If you know
I've been cursed and warned, then you must know about the
two demons; you could only know about them if you are
one of them!" The chapel was empty; he went to the altar
rail and fell to his knees; holding his hands he began to pray
for God's help, hopeful that everything Jeanie was saying
was some kind of hoax, a sophisticated joke being played
on a country boy. She knelt next to him while he prayed and
continued telling her yarn. "Healing people is God's way of
telling you that you've been picked to be an invocator."

He ended his prayer and stood up. Turning to her he said,
"I don't want to have anything to do with you anymore." She
responded, "You have no choice; I'm never going to leave
you."

That evening he felt more confused than ever. He decided it might help him if he met with her again. It was late,
after 11 p.m. Ignoring the 10 p.m. curfew, he went out a back
service door and walked the twenty or so blocks to the very
substantial mansion home of Jeanie's master. He was not accustomed to breaking rules; however he insisted on doing
whatever needed to be done to get out of his horrifying pre-
dicament.

The butler, an elderly man, was not amused at greeting a
guest at such a late hour. "I need to see Jeanie; it's very important." Unsmiling, he looked Ephriam over. He was a tall,
very dark black man, impeccably dressed in a blue suit; the
light from the chandelier reflected off his shiny hairless head.
"Jeanie Belvoir is a servant girl here; she stays here when
her duties require it. She isn't allowed to receive guests."
Just then the lady of the house, Mrs. Ganter, entered the vestibule, curious who had knocked on the door. The very attractive, tall shapely woman with her gray hair pinned back
into a twist was wearing an expensive long green robe over

her night clothing. "Ma'am, please forgive me. My name is Ephriam Bernharter; I'm a student at the seminary. I had a very intense conversation with your servant Jeanie Belvoir today, and I need to talk to her a bit more. Its very important to me, I hope you understand."

The woman was becoming increasingly irritated because of the late visit. "Where do you know Jeanie from? Are you a bounty hunter? She's a free colored." He tried to reason with the socialite. "We're close friends; may I please see her?" The butler interrupted, "Madam, I'll go and get the authorities." She responded with a clipped sentence. "No, I'm going to let him see her." She turned to him and gave him his instructions. "The servant's wing is to your left, Charles will take you to her room. You have ten minutes to say whatever you have to say, and then get out of my house. I would suggest that you not have colored girls as friends."

Shocked when Jeanie saw him, she grabbed his arm and pulled him into her room, a small, cramped closet with just enough space for a cot and chair. "You are out of your mind! What brings you here? What do you want? I could lose my job over this!" He was frazzled, the look of despair on his face clearly revealed how disturbed he was. "I must rid myself of this terrible marking." She lost her patience; she had enough of it all. "Live with it; give up trying to change things!" Weary, he collapsed on her bed. "Please let me rest for a few minutes, then I'll leave. I don't want to get you into more trouble." He was so tired he fell into a deep sleep.

About two hours later he was awakened with her on top of him nude; he tried to get to his feet but he couldn't move. He was paralyzed! He was shocked into disbelief; she was a demon! He could feel that he was inside her, she was quietly laughing, moving up and down on his penis while raping him, a haze of blue smoke coming out of her ears, nose, and the corners of her mouth. A "normal" erection, a natural type that he had achieved with Catherine, was nothing like this experience. His penis was so hard and erect it felt like it was made of stone. He reached down and felt it between her thrusts; it had been turned into a rod of polished granite! He had no sensation; he felt nothing. There was no fear of premature ejaculation, he was sure she wasn't going to allow him to have an orgasm until she was ready to have hers; three hours later she decided to stop. He became ill after he exploded in her. The thought of his semen living inside a demon caused him to roll over and hang his head over the bed's edge and vomit on the floor.

Ephriam was naturally curious about sex; before he knew what Jeanie really was he thought about how it would be to have sexual relations with her; he had dreamed of the pleasure they could give to each other. He had hesitated pursuing her in that way not because she was black; he didn't want to ruin what he thought was a very special friendship uncomplicated by romance and sex; they had talked for hours sharing their ideas and thoughts. But it was indeed all ruined now. He had to live for the rest of his life with the memory of having been inside a demon.

She was a whore. She was all things vile and despicable. Ephriam said, "You don't look like a demon; you don't look like Daytrin who came to my room at Swatara Academy or that disgusting creature Balair." She laughed. "Would you have become my friend if I looked like Daytrin or Balair?" She threatened him again. "We will always be able to share our fucking. Perhaps someday when you're married I can tell your wife all about it; that's if you give me reason. Then again, perhaps she might walk into the bedroom while we're fucking so hard that the whole bed is shaking!" He couldn't find the energy to confront her. "The reason I fucked you was to show you I can do anything I want to you and to anybody or anything that is important to you. Remember, I will never be leaving you." He had overstayed his visit and he knew he had to get out of the house without Mrs. Ganter or Charles the butler noticing, and he knew he had to resist Jeanie, but she kept talking. "You might very well have a wife, children, and a congregation, but you will never live one second on Earth without Jeanie Belvoir!"

During those long conversations late into the night he had always seen a pleasing, gentle smile on her face. Her eyes would twinkle with joy and excitement, anxiously contemplating his next words and observations. It was all an act; he had been foolish; he had been duped. Now her gentle and friendly words could quickly turn into snarls from curled lips that were becoming part of a twisted and distorted face unveiling the look of hatred. Words flowing from her gentle feminine voice could easily change into deep and low growling pronunciations. "Never doubt that I'll do whatever I need to do to keep you within my reach, to watch your every move, to make sure you don't do whatever God has planned for you." Ephriam doubted she could totally control him. "I'll resist you. My life will unfold without your interference!" She roared with laughter. "You have no power to stop me. I raped you because I wanted to, and I can bring tragedy to your life with a blink of my eyes, a snap of my fingers, a nod, a blown kiss." Ephriam risked her wrath, telling her defiantly that Jesus Christ was his savior who would deliver him from her evil.

"Jesus won't deliver you from my evil because you aren't going to ask him. You have too much to lose if you deny me; I can destroy the people and the things you love. I control your sister Anne; a part of Satan lives in her, Balair put Satan in her when he took her by the hand and walked her into that park along the river, a pit of evil that keeps so many despicable secrets under its veil of darkness. I can call on her to serve Satan at anytime. I can kill her in a second perhaps by a massive stroke or heart failure. After I destroy her I'll expect your gratitude for me bringing her a merciful demise instead of suffering from a painful, agonizing death."

"You can be stopped from doing God's work beyond the pulpit." Ephriam jumped in. "Hah, beyond the pulpit? I can certainly do much of God's work from the pulpit!" Jeanie had a quick answer. "You can be watched when you're in the pulpit, preaching to people who aren't listening, daydreaming about what's for Sunday dinner. In the pulpit you're wasting your breath; you're harmless!"

Ephriam lunged for her, but fell down, and as she looked down at him she spat on him. He looked up into that awful face of hatred. He was getting scared; now he believed everything Jeanie was saying. He kept quiet while she continued to have plenty to say. "I can put part of Satan inside your mother and I can have your father succumb to adultery, to thievery, to rape, to murder. I can put Satan inside your future wife and your children. I can have a bear eat your son or your daughter. I can have your wife raped and then murdered. I can start a house fire in a whim; I can burn a whole family to death in seconds. If you betray me, I'll ruin your life. I'll do whatever I must do to make you obey me. I can control, manipulate, and destroy anyone that you love or care for; I can send them all to Hell!"

"What am I supposed to do, what do you expect from me?" She had a ready answer. "All you must do to keep me happy is to warn me if any event or calling from God occurs. I've been sent into your life to make sure you don't help God perform a miracle. It's that simple."

He again suspected this was all a mistake; he had received his calling to preach, and he believed he had prayers answered, but other than that he'd never had a vision or message from God. She said, "Come to terms with your plight! Just because you haven't had a vision or message, doesn't mean you won't get one. You might never get one, you might get one next month, next year, ten or twenty or thirty years from now."

Ephriam was practically convinced Jeanie had the power to follow through with her threats if he didn't obey her. However, he still had questions. She said, "You'll find out what you need to know when you need to know."

Ephriam was exhausted; he just wanted to get out of the mansion before the police were contacted. He didn't want to hear anymore from her, but she added. "Don't ever mention this special relationship that exists between you and me, and don't conspire against me, don't ignore me, don't make me angry. If you do I'll strike back."

He had never doubted his faith in God could bring him through any crisis, but now he felt he was on the brink of a nervous breakdown. He was in a state of deep depression, spending three days alone in his room without food or drink. He feigned migraine headaches to avoid going to class. He emerged from exile convinced that everything Jeanie told him is truthful and that he must live with this awful situation that evidently is his destiny.

A week later he found the courage to go back to the mansion and risk Jeanie's further wrath because he had more questions to ask her. Charles the butler explained, "Jeanie Belvoir works here at the Ganter residence, but she only stays over when she is scheduled to watch the children on early mornings." Charles looked over his shoulder, making sure Mr. or Mrs. Ganter weren't watching or within earshot, then whispered Jeanie's address.

Ephriam traveled by coach two or three miles or so to a poor black neighborhood on the edge of the city. At the address Charles gave him, he found an empty, filthy, barren room, with its sagging door half open and window frames covered with spider webs. The room was in the cellar of a small used harness shop. He asked the shop owner, a very old man, if he had seen his tenant. He was hunchbacked and deaf; he obviously hadn't worked in years. "Tenant? What tenant? The last time I had a tenant in the cellar was twenty years ago." Ephriam, needing to speak loudly, confirmed the address. "Huh, yea that's it, but the only people who lived in the room were my apprentices. I never would rent to a woman, too many problems doing that!" After thanking the old man for his time, he asked the grocer across the street, the baker in the next block, the milkman doing his deliveries, and a few of the neighbors walking about, if they knew where he could find her. He described her to them. No one had seen Jeanie Belvoir. They never heard of a Jeanie Belvoir!

Chapter 11

1840

Ephriam meets Gretchen

Ephriam never had enough money to travel very far from Philadelphia, not to the New Jersey seashore, or to the Catskills to the North. Henry would send him spending money, and Sally would save some money from her household fund and forward it to him whenever she could. Both his parents made sure he had train fare to get home for holidays. Since he no longer had Jeanie around, on weekends he would join some of his classmates and take the trolley to the outskirts of Philadelphia and stroll through the various parks playing outdoor games and running foot races. He particularly enjoyed walking along the riverbank. During many of these weekends Lutheran families would invite the divinity students to their homes for Sunday dinner and recitals or other evening entertainment.

On a cold, sunny Sunday morning in October, Ephriam attended Reformation Sunday services in one of the larger and more affluent Lutheran churches. After the service, church council president John Stanton pulled him aside. "I've been told you are the grandson of Reverend Luther Bernharter." Ephriam proudly acknowledged he was. "My family and I would like you to come for Sunday dinner." Stanton was pleased when Ephriam gladly accepted the invitation. "A young, hard working divinity student should be rewarded with German foods that my wife Francine prepares."

As they got into the carriage Ephriam was further rewarded. John and Francine Stanton's beautiful daughter Gretchen was among the Stanton family members joining them. She had light chestnut brown hair piled atop her head, looking at the same time prepared and spontaneous; curls, some springy, some relaxed, were falling down along both sides of her beautiful petite face that featured sensuous lips and glossy light blue eyes. She was dressed in a beautiful and obviously expensive purple satin ruffled dress, with a pale orange bonnet. The pleasant, subtle smell of her perfume filled the carriage.

Her beauty captivated him; he had to remind himself the entire afternoon not to stare at her across the table or the room; he couldn't keep his eyes off of her. She noticed his flirting and occasionally responded with a brief glance and a smile.

Instead of visiting an assortment of Philadelphia churches to worship and learn the preaching techniques of different pastors, he began attending the Stanton's church every Sunday just to see her. Many weekday evenings he traveled the long 45 minute trolley trip back and forth just so he could see her at church meetings and social events, or occasionally at the museum where she was a volunteer guide, or at the library for book readings she attended regularly. Gretchen was friendly, but she was a shy girl. She was only seventeen years old and a member of a very proper, conservative family. She was not ready to be courted, and Ephriam was in no position to be courting a girl anyway.

He had hoped someday to court her, and when spring was approaching, just before her eighteenth birthday, she finally consented to a brief meeting for coffee on a Saturday afternoon in the parlor of her parent's home. For him it had been love at first sight. He was sure it was not just an infatuation, but the beginning of a deep, long lasting love.

Of course he had to consider his problems. His ability to heal, his sexual experience with Jeanie, her threats, Daytrin and Balair's intrusions and warnings, and Anne's well being, were all hurdles in his life that was becoming more and more complicated. A woman contemplating marrying him should be told about these perils; he would hardly blame her for running away as fast has her legs could carry her.

He decided he would tell her about his life's hazards later. Gretchen was very cautious, very proper. Although she occasionally could be talkative, she was rarely outgoing, especially when her parents weren't present; when it came to boys she chose to move very slowly. Ephriam was relieved she was in no hurry to marry. He had two more years of college ahead of him. He could lose her if she decided to pursue marriage sooner; an older man who already had his career started could come along and sweep her up, stealing her from right under Ephriam's nose.

May and the end of his sophomore year arrived. He was going to miss her, at the same time he was eager to go home and spend the summer with his family and friends.

He got home on Saturday evening, tired from the long train ride. He was anxious to hear his grandfather preach again. When he entered the church that Sunday morning he got a wonderful surprise. Sitting in a pew with her father and mother and another family was Gretchen!

She was laughing and full of excitement. He had never seen her that happy. "I've kept this secret from you for so long! My aunt and uncle live in Farntown, and back at Christmas time they had invited my parents to visit. They helped me make it a surprise visit for you!" Farntown, the next town over, was only two miles East of Hamlin. Ephriam had assumed when he first met John Stanton that he knew his grandfather from his guest preaching in Philadelphia. He had attended many of Luther Bernharter's Philadelphia services, but he knew him long before as his sister's minister.

This ironic connection made it possible for the young couple to spend time together in Philadelphia and Farntown, avoiding long separations during Ephriam's semester breaks and summer vacations. Eventually Gretchen's parents allowed her to travel alone to visit her aunt and uncle and cousins, and to be near Ephriam. When she was staying in Farntown, he was with her everyday. At church services they were allowed to sit together. He would help her bake cookies; they would take long walks, go on picnics, go fishing, and swim in Lake Stamen, located on the Eastern edge of Hamlin along the road to Farntown. The lake was small, about fifteen acres, surrounded by woods except on the South shore where the road running from Farntown West to Hamlin passed by. There were small cottages along the wooded Northwestern shore, the furthermost from the road.

He started getting strange thoughts again about the lake since going there with Gretchen. When he was growing up he always had an eerie feeling about the lake. One frigid and windy winter night when he was twelve years old, while walking home from Farntown, he passed by and noticed there was moonlight aglow over the water, but the moon was nowhere to be seen in the very black sky. He got scared; he was tempted to run as fast as his legs would carry him. Instead, bolstered by a surge of courage, he walked out on the dock, knelt down, and put his hand in the water. He quickly pulled it out; the lake was as warm as bathwater! Now, spending the warm summertime there with Gretchen, the water seemed to have a soothing effect on both of them; they blamed the euphoria on their being in love, but Ephriam suspected it was more than that. After being in the water he seemed intoxicated with a heightened appreciation of all things good and thoughts of ridding people of their misfortunes. Sitting with her on the old, broken down boat dock, he confessed how he felt. "I think maybe there is some supernatural influence swirling around in this water." Gretchen laughed while watching him stare out over the calm water with its occasional ripple from a leaping frog or fish. "You are studying to be a minister, but you treat your enthusiasm about life as a 'supernatural influence.' What about thanking God for blessing you with inspiration to love life and offer help to the poor!" He appreciated her attempt at a logical explanation; perhaps he was just paranoid considering his past experiences, experiences Gretchen didn't know anything about. "I'm sure it's more than that, maybe someday I'll explain to you why I feel the way I do."

He was convinced he and Gretchen would marry someday. He couldn't resist wondering if God led him to Gretchen, or her to him. If it were God's plan he would be forever grateful; he would be the happiest man that ever lived. If Satan had brought him Gretchen, if Jeanie or Daytrin, or Balair, were responsible for her entering is life, he knew there would be a horrible price to pay. He had watched for signs of the blue haze coming from her. He had not seen any.

Back in Philadelphia, Ephriam was now allowed to officially court Gretchen. They would attend services at many churches; hearing different pastors preach helped him develop his own style. After the worship services he would introduce himself to the minister, telling them he was a seminary student. Since he started attending seminary he would accept their invitations to attend church meetings and social events, to help with the worship service, and to teach Sunday school. With his church activities, plus spending time courting Gretchen and keeping up with his demanding studies, he found himself in the same situation when he was spending hours with Jeanie, there was scarcely enough time to sleep.

Gretchen met him at the seminary library one evening to help him prepare for a difficult examination. When the library closed they waited outside for the Stanton carriage to pick her up. During the conversation, she asked him if he had noticed that her brother had been born with a bad left arm; he couldn't lift it over his head, and it was slightly shorter that his right arm. Gretchen explained to him that when the arm becomes inflamed every few days it causes her brother to endure awful pain.

The next evening while the two of them were having dinner at a small, quaint restaurant frequented regularly by the Stanton family, he revealed to her his secret. "If you want me to, I'll lay my hands on your brother's arm and pray for him; it might help." He got worried when he saw the startled look on her face. "I don't talk about this special power, if in fact that is what it is. If people knew about it they'd make fun of me; they'd call me a freak trying to be like God." Gretchen recovered. "What does the seminary think about all this?" He nervously scrutinized the dining room, searching for anyone who might overhear the conversation. He whispered, "They know nothing about it and they can never know anything about it! My mental health would be questioned; I would be subjected to psychological testing and evaluation. They would conspire to expel me; the church frowns on people who claim to have the ability to heal. They teach that only Jesus Christ, the Son of God, ever healed the sick, blind, and infirm."

†

Chapter 12

1840

Ephriam prays for Gretchen's brother

Ephriam told Gretchen the details about his gift; he assured her he always planned to tell her and that he would never keep such an important part of his life from her. Asking a woman to be a pastor's wife was sacrifice enough. Now she would have to cope with the burden of keeping this secret her entire life.

She indeed wanted him to see her brother and maybe help him, but Ephriam feared there was a chance he would lose her if her brother didn't respond. If his prayers failed to make a difference, she could become one of those people who would laugh at him, mock him, and gossip. She would break his heart. It was a gamble he was forced to make; he was confident the odds were in his favor right now.

Of course Ephriam didn't share with her the much bigger secret. Convinced she wouldn't believe him, he selfishly denied her the knowledge that he was cursed by demons and warned not to heal anyone. He decided not to tell her she was being exposed to possible calamity.

Jimmy Stanton was a bitter man, never smiling, not at all friendly. He was skinny, weighing maybe 150 pounds soaking wet, with thin, straight brown hair that he combed straight back. His beak nose and small chin made him unattractive. He was a member of a family of beautiful women and handsome men. Somehow Jimmy got shortchanged. He used his arm and how people discriminated against him as an excuse not to work. The Stantons, blaming themselves for his suffering, allowed him to sit around and sulk. They wondered if his affliction was God's punishment for some sinful act a family member had committed years or generations ago. Gretchen didn't believe any of that; she warned Ephriam not to get baited and reeled into such irrational notions if asked.

Gretchen told Jimmy her boyfriend was a seminary student and was willing to touch his arm and pray for him. He snapped at her, "Don't waste my time with such foolishness! And don't go talking about your invalid brother to others; it's none of anybody's business!"

Eventually, after a few months of visiting, engaging in good conversation with Mr. Stanton and eating Gretchen and her mother's cooking, Jimmy warmed up ever so slightly to Ephriam, at least as much as Jimmy ever warmed up to anybody. Now, at least, he would engage in some checked conversation and make occasional eye contact. One Sunday after dinner while the entire family sat in the parlor, Ephriam and Jimmy stayed in the dining room. Gretchen whispered, "Jimmy, why don't you let Ephriam hold your arm for a minute?" She went into the parlor with the other family members, leaving the two men alone. Jimmy stared across the room at the future minister. He kept staring, not knowing how to ask. Ephriam stayed seated; he didn't want to pressure the headstrong man. Finally Jimmy got up and walked across the room and held out his left hand; Ephriam reached up and clasped it. A look of shock came across Jimmy's face when he felt the tingling in his arm while Ephriam was holding it. Ephriam endured his heart fluttering and breathlessness;

he learned how to conceal it somewhat. He spoke softly. "I can't cure your arm Jimmy, but I think the pain won't be as bad now."

Gretchen told Jimmy not to mention Ephriam's healing powers to anyone. It could get him expelled from the seminary.

Jimmy began to notice a difference in his arm a few days later; he was relieved of much of the pain. Ephriam continued to hold his arm every few weeks. After years of suffering, Jimmy now realized he had reasons to live. He started working at a dry goods store near the Stanton home. For the rest of his life he would be grateful for the help his soon to be brother-in-law gave him.

Gretchen and Ephriam were now very much in love and devoted to each other. They had known each other for almost a year. Marriage was out of the question for now. Ephriam knew he needed to finish school, get ordained, and get appointed pastor of a church somewhere to begin his career.

Ephriam didn't consider himself the most handsome man. He had rough features, brown hair and eyes; he was broad shouldered and broad wasted like his father and grandfather. But he knew Gretchen's beauty was the type that would remain with her all of her life. She got her beauty from her mother, who was radiant and natural. Ephriam watched as she helped her parents greet influential guests for a Saturday brunch. Her alabaster skin and long light brown hair, along with her sparkling blue eyes made her almost mirage like while she stood in the sunlight shining through the window. Her parents could afford to give her the best clothes; she chose simple dresses, mostly solid colored, but many with flowery prints. She wore very little jewelry, usually a simple necklace with a cross or heart shaped pendant.

Ephriam's insecurities when it came to romance were exasperated by Gretchen's reserve. He said, "I sometimes lay awake at night wondering if you really love me as much as I love you." She usually had to search for words when they were having this type of intimate conversation. Finally she would softly whisper, "I love you more than ever, I want to spend my life with you."

Ephriam had to believe her. He wasn't the same innocent boy that was in love with Miss Noll, that young man who left Hamlin for Swatara Academy. He wanted serious commitment from the girl he planned to have children with and spend the rest of his life with. For now the commitment he was willing to settle for was simple statements professing her love.

Then he came to realize that because he worshipped her he had difficulty thinking of her sexually; sex would ruin her, losing her virginity would spoil her pure body and spirit. He knew these thoughts had the potential to harm him psychologically, so he quickly fantasized about an antidote. He would test her; he would demand they sleep together! He would tell her he just wanted to make love to her once before their marriage. It would relieve him of the anxiety he will surely feel on their wedding night. They both would be experienced at lovemaking, she would know what to expect. He could perform the romantic role assigned to him more confidently.

Maybe he could just ask her to take her clothes off and allow him to see her naked. Then when they kissed she would allow him to briefly feel her bare breasts. She certainly wouldn't mind him kissing her bare breasts would she? And how about her vagina? Maybe she would let him touch her bare breasts and her vagina. If she really loved him, shouldn't she be willing to make him happy?

Then he came to his senses and realized Gretchen would be devastated if he suggested these things that evolved from the wicked thoughts that swirled around in his mind. She had nothing to worry about. He had become a man of patience and good character; he was good enough to deliver the word of God from the pulpit and man enough to lay with Gretchen Stanton in their marriage bed. He considered himself the luckiest man in the world.

In a rare moment of melancholy, he confided in his roommate, Michael Herbine. He was a strange fellow, and up until now Ephriam had limited his contact with him, only exchanging the normal courtesies and pleasantries necessary for roommates to cohabitate.

Michael was a loner. He studied hard, prayed hard, and the rest of the time had his head in a book. He even read in the dining hall while eating his meals. He was a good-looking young man, brown hair and eyes, slender and of medium height. He was average in every way. He wore spectacles; he had two suits that he wore on alternating days.

"I get frustrated with my girlfriend. She is so beautiful and I'm so in love with her." Ephriam had started talking to him while he was reading yet another book. Ephriam actually didn't expect any response, but he did look up; evidently hearing the word girlfriend caught his attention. "When you say frustrated, you mean sexually don't you?" Ephriam said, "No! I don't mean it the way you think I do. I mean, I just want to be married so I can make love to her."

Michael continued, "I know what you are going through. I have a girl back home; we're going to be engaged next year. You probably think I'm some sort of social misfit." Ephriam kept to himself that very idea. He said, "Well then I guess you know what I'm going through."

Michael gave him some advice. "Do what I do every month, go down to the river district and visit one of the whorehouses." Ephriam was surprised to hear that suggestion. "Seminary students aren't supposed to patronize prostitutes! We're going to be men of God." Michael laughed. "Yes, I know. It's a sin. Are you going to wait for me to admit I'm a sinner for going there?"

Ephriam always tried to avoid judging other people. "No,

I'm sure you already know all that. I just didn't think you engaged in such behavior." Michael said, "Such behavior? Look, don't make life so complicated. You are a young man trying to live a virtuous life, but you got needs, needs that all young men have. Just because you are going to be a minister doesn't mean you don't have those needs." Ephriam said, "We're supposed to hold ourselves to a higher standard."

Michael, not the type to debate, put his face back into his book. Ephriam interrupted him again. "When are you going down there again? How much does it cost? Will you take me along next time?"

Michael replied, "It costs $2. I'm going Friday night when my allowance comes, and yes, you can go along." Ephriam plopped down on his bed as if he made one of the most serious decisions of his young life. Michael replied, "And don't try to convert any of those whores, they'll laugh their asses off at you."

They walked along the narrow dark street until they came to this tiny, run down house crammed into a row of quite a few others. They were old houses, only about twelve feet wide, probably built years ago for the families of seamen. They at first appeared to be clones, but the different paint colors of the shutters and doorways, and the shingles on the roof, made them all unique. There was a light in the window. While Michael knocked on the door Ephriam bent over to look inside, but the sheer curtains, intended to leave light inside during daytime, were thick enough to distort the image of anybody or anything in the front room. An old woman, her appearance shockingly grotesque, answered the door. She wore orange rouge on her deep wrinkled cheeks, and thick red lipstick haphazardly painted all around her mouth and black, rotting teeth. She wore a multi-colored patchwork blanket draped over her obviously very large 300-pound body.

She knew Michael by name; he was indeed, as he had said, a regular client. "I brought along a friend, he's my roommate. I hope you don't mind. His name is Ephriam." He noticed how stiff and quiet Ephriam had become. "This is Rose, she's the madam." Rose invited them inside, and then turned and asked, "You boys aren't homosexuals are you?" Ephriam quickly said he was not; he wondered why she would care if they were.

She called two girls into the room. Ephriam's heart was racing; he had a bad case of a quivering stomach. Michael gave Rose $2 and pointed to the girl standing to the left. Ephriam paid Rose and the other girl took his hand. They walked through the kitchen to a very small room at the back of the house just large enough to accommodate the single bed. A gas lamp hung from the ceiling. She was about thirty years old, short and slender, with short-cropped brown hair. She had that sexy look that some women have; she had a pretty face, small breasts and perfect legs. She was a girl that could easily drive men to fight for her, that is if she hadn't decided for some reason to become a prostitute. "You'll have to excuse me, I'm a little nervous. What's your name?" Without answering him, she sat unsmiling on the edge of the bed and started to unbuckle his belt. As soon as his trousers fell to the floor she began fondling him; he quickly became erect. She unbuttoned her dress and slid back on the bed, laying down and spreading her legs. Ephriam knew it was all up to him now. He lay down on top of her, and as soon as he entered her, she pushed and pulled, heaving rapidly; he was finished in five seconds! He got to his feet after she squirmed to get out from under him. He was still buttoning his trousers and buckling his belt while she was pulling him along the hall back to the front room where two other men were awaiting their turn. He met Michael outside. "How about we go for a beer to celebrate your first visit to a whorehouse!" Ephriam said, "That sounds like a good idea, let's celebrate my first *and* last visit to a whorehouse!"

Chapter 13

1841

Graduation, ordination, marriage, and installation

In a gala outdoor ceremony on the large, rolling campus lawn, Ephriam walked to the front of his classmates and their families and friends and received his diploma. That sunny and breezy June day in 1841 commenced the beginning of what he hoped would be a long and successful career preaching the Gospel and ministering to a congregation.

It was Henry Bernharter's proudest day. Henry, Sally and Anne were guests of the Stantons for the two days they were in Philadelphia. Grandfather Luther was invited to stand on the stage and shake his grandson's hand after the dean of students gave him his diploma.

They were hectic weeks leading up to Ephriam's wonderful day. A frenzied atmosphere reigned: day after day of church services, rehearsals, prayers, the fitting of robes, and what felt like an endless amount of receptions held for and by dignitaries, alumni, and visiting pastors, along with numerous organizations whom contributed to the support of the school.

A final, private reception was held in the Stanton home with only members and close friends of both families in attendance.

Two days earlier Ephriam had told Gretchen that he planned to ask her father for his daughter's hand in marriage at the family gathering. Gretchen talked him out of doing that. "That evening is going to be the culmination of your wonderful day. It's going to be about you and what you have accomplished in your young life. I don't want that day to be anything but a celebration of your graduation." He relented. "But I am so anxious for everyone to know that we are going to be married."

She smiled and took his hand and gently squeezed it. "I think you are forgetting a very important part of our being engaged." He looked puzzled. "What am I forgetting?" She answered while laughing. "Ephriam, you never asked me to marry you!" His startled look caused her to laugh even more, and soon an inquisitive look and faint smile was painted on his face. Ephriam and Gretchen had fallen so much in love that their marriage was assumed to be inevitable by both of them and their families and friends; a natural progression of their relationship. "I'm sorry, I just never thought to formally propose to you, but I'm not taking you for granted; when I daydream about my future it always includes you by my side. You will marry me, won't you?" Gretchen replied, "Is that your proposal?" Ephriam realized that he was making a bad situation worse. He got serious; he looked deep into her eyes, took her hand and asked, "Gretchen, will you marry me?" She smiled gently. "Yes, Ephriam, I will marry you."

The frenzy caused by a graduation was now going to be replaced by a much larger celebration, the marriage of Gretchen Stanton. Because the Stantons were a distinguished Philadelphia family, the marriage of their daughter would be a major social event. The work involved to pull it off was overwhelming. The Stanton's housekeeping staff was put to work preparing meals, sewing gowns, and assisting with accommodating guests who stayed over while helping with the preliminary social events leading up to the actual wedding.

On Saturday, September 11, 1841, Ephriam and Gretchen were married in the seminary's chapel with Reverend Frank Herr, Ephriam's cherished mentor, officiating; grandfather Luther Bernharter assisted. It was a Lutheran service with all the old world formality and tradition that a wedding held at a seminary for the daughter of a socially prominent family could include. The list of guests included many dignitaries: the mayor of Philadelphia, numerous patrons of the arts, business leaders and their families, along with the extended family members and many close friends. Newspaper reporters were welcomed and accommodated. John Stanton had chartered a train car to bring the Bernharter and Stanton family members and friends to Philadelphia and paid for hotel accommodations for all of them.

Everyone attending the major social event was fashionably dressed. The women were bedecked in expensive jewelry; they wore their elegant gowns, parasols, and fancy colorfully plumed hats. The men were dressed in their finest dark wool suits.

The elegant, formal wedding's music included Mendelssohn's *Wedding March,* Bach's *Jesu, Joy of Man's Desiring,* and the great Lutheran hymn by Martin Luther, which many consider to be the best ever written:

Did we in our own strength confide, our striving would be losing;
Were not the right Man on our side, the Man of God's own choosing:
Dost ask who that may be? Christ Jesus, it is He;
Lord Sabaoth, His Name, from age to age the same,
And He must win the battle.

Gretchen's attendants; her schoolmates and Anne, wore fine gowns of tangerine taffeta with high necklines and puffy sleeves with matching picture hats; they carried bouquets of white carnations.

Gretchen wore a traditional white-veiled wedding gown

with a long train and puffy sleeves. Her hair was pinned up and pulled back from her face; she wore soft subtle makeup and long dangling pear-shaped earrings. She was a beautiful bride.

The men wore dark suits. Ephriam had chosen three of his classmates from seminary as his attendants.

Immediately after the ceremony a grand luncheon was celebrated at the country club where John Stanton was a member. Grand carriages with uniformed teamsters and footmen transported the invited guests to the inn about five miles from the seminary.

That evening an extravagant reception was held on the lawn of the Stanton estate. Tables were set up in large tents with attendants serving food and drink. Flaming torchlights lit up the area.

Ephriam never imagined that Gretchen had so many aunts, uncles and cousins. His head was buzzing from all the introductions and reminiscing. Practically every one of them insisted on telling him about some incident in Gretchen's life that they had, to their recollection, a prominent role in. There were plenty of Bernharters there also, but they were far out-numbered. The standout Bernharter, of course, was the most distinguished guest of all, the Reverend Luther Bernharter. He always attracted a crowd with his outrageously funny stories, always with a moral or anecdote, and a reminder that the groom was his grandson. A trio seated on the flagstone deck consisting of a violinist, cellist and pianist performed wedding music throughout the evening.

The bride and groom spent a week at Cape May, New Jersey before returning to Philadelphia. John and Francine Stanton insisted they stay in the Stanton guest cottage until Ephriam found a position.

The newlyweds were anxious for Ephriam to find a church to serve. Grandfather Luther had dreamed of his grandson preaching from the same pulpit he preached from for thirty-two years. As Ephriam's ordination came close, the retired pastor asked his replacement, Mark Randolph, if he would consider taking the young man on as an assistant pastor. Randolph wasn't willing to do this because he was of the opinion that the small congregation couldn't afford to pay two pastors. He was probably right. What he was willing to do, however, was accept an appointment to the diocese hierarchy if it was offered to him, something that he knew the old man could make happen. Randolph got his appointment, and now the members of St. Luke's Lutheran Church in Hamlin, Ephriam's home church, were given the opportunity to hold a congregational vote to call Reverend Ephriam Bernharter as their third pastor.

For Ephriam, it was a dream that came true. He had always believed God would someday let him be pastor of St. Luke's, but he didn't expect it to happen until he got some years of experience. He and Gretchen were overjoyed, but he began to feel some guilt knowing that his calling was a result of his grandfather's powerful influence.

He and Gretchen traveled back to Hamlin so he could meet with his grandfather, who lived West of the square, across the road from the church, just three blocks from Henry and Sally's house. Rachael Bernharter was a wonderful grandmother; she always had cookies to offer her grandson. When he was a little boy she would watch his eyes fixate on the cookie jar as soon as he entered her kitchen. His face would light up with a broad smile that only a boy enjoying her delicious baked treats could put on view. Rachael was a gracious hostess to everyone, but when Ephriam visited it was such a special occasion to her and to him.

However, he had always felt uneasy visiting with his grandfather. Luther Bernharter was a large man, over six feet tall, a broad waste line, and an imposing baritone voice. No back pew churchgoer ever complained they couldn't hear the word of God when he preached. He was an imposing man;

he always wore his charcoal suit, his pocket watch chain dangling from his vest pocket. He smoked good cigars, and they perfumed his clothing and the overstuffed furniture and carpeting in his study. When Henry and Sally visited when Ephriam was small, he felt secure sitting next to his father while the old man lectured; he didn't mind the admonitions because they were directed to his father.

Then later, beginning when he was in his teens, he found it necessary on certain occasions to come by alone. Visits on his birthday were necessary; presenting his grades from Miss Noll, and later Swatara Academy was a requirement. He no longer had his father by his side to represent him, to defend him.

He was always jittery when it was time to walk down the hallway leading to the study. He would control himself by starting to count the enormous number of books on the shelves that lined the walls, causing Luther to admonish him for not paying attention to what was being said.

Now it was time for him to be a man, to behave like a fellow minister, to speak up and explain what was on his mind. "Sir, I have misgivings about accepting St. Luke's call because of your influence playing a major role in my getting the job." Luther just stared across his big walnut desk, through the haze of cigar smoke, at his grandson's face, the sunshine from the window illuminating it. Then he spoke. "Ephriam, influence is what gets you anywhere and everywhere. You need to be here at your home doing God's work." Ephriam expected that answer. "I want to be here, but I want to get a calling based on my own qualifications, not because of your manipulations." He didn't want to disappoint his mother and father, or his grandparents, but he felt relieved now that he said how he felt.

He had been looking forward to a great life leading a congregation, preaching in the pulpit every Sunday, serving communion to the parishioners, baptizing their infants, marrying them, and yes, presiding at their funerals, all the while being near and among his and Gretchen's families. Gretchen's parents were preparing to purchase a summerhouse at Lake Stamen. They were planning to spend many weeks, and eventually all summer, at the house to be near their daughter, her husband, and the grandchildren.

Now he had misgivings. Luther said, "Very well, give me your letter declining the appointment, and I'll present it to church council. They can begin searching for a pastor." Ephriam was taken aback from his grandfather's reaction. He expected to get a reprimand, to get chastised for refusing such an opportunity. He expected to be criticized for not thinking of his wife, his family, her family, and the little country church that wanted their favorite son to lead them. "Ephriam, you have never been a selfish man, but you are being selfish now. But you do as you wish, you do what you think you must do, but don't expect me to agree. You are being very foolish; go on now and live with your mistakes." Luther got up from his leather desk chair to expedite his grandson's departure, trying his very best to hide his anger.

Ephriam didn't sleep well that night. He thought that perhaps he was being ungrateful. Was he being selfish? Was he a fool? He looked at Gretchen sleeping next to him, she looked so beautiful and at peace. He felt a lot of weight on his shoulders. He was aware of the responsibility he had to provide Gretchen with a good life. She was a rich man's daughter. She was raised in privilege. He could never give her a life her parents lived; he knew she understood that. She wanted to be a pastor's wife with all the good and bad things that go with that life. But he did need to provide her with a comfortable lifestyle and a prominent place in whatever community they chose to become part of. He also wanted his parents to be proud of him. He wanted to help and protect dear Anne. It would be a difficult decision to turn down the opportunity that was presented to him no matter how it came to be.

Unable to sleep, he walked to his grandparent's house and sat on the porch bench waiting for sunrise. Rachael noticed her grandson sleeping on the bench when she opened the curtains to allow the sun into the parlor. "Luther, I think you are going to have an early guest." He looked out the window and shook his head. "Rachael, he is a very complicated fellow."

He knocked on the door and asked to see his grandfather. Rachael said, "Why don't you have some breakfast first; you'll feel better if you have something in your stomach." Ephriam replied, "Grandma, I have never gone into that study with anything in my stomach, and I'm not about to begin doing so now!" Walking down the hall he worked on his courage as the cigar smell increased. He didn't sit down; he chose to stand. "I will be honored to accept the call as pastor of St. Luke's Lutheran Church, Hamlin, Pennsylvania." Luther took a drag from his morning cigar, leaned forward, took a sip of his coffee, and then looked up at the young man standing before him. "You and your wife move into that big house with your parents and then get to work."

In return for him working very hard, working long hours, bonding with each family's young and old and their joys and sorrows and sickness and health, the people of St. Luke's would take care of him and Gretchen, and their children. They would reward them with the security and comforts needed for a long and peaceful life.

A proud Henry and Sally Bernharter, just recently celebrating their son's graduation and marriage, now walked the two blocks for church services. There were two special ceremonies held two weeks apart; his ordination as a Lutheran minister, and his installation as pastor of St. Luke's Lutheran Church.

Chapter 14

1843

A baby is born, and Jeanie returns

For the next two years their lives were very busy. Not only was Ephriam performing his basic duties as a pastor, but Gretchen was busy meeting challenges and effecting accomplishments that never occurred to her as a young girl. The home visitations and dinner invitations allowed her little time to practice her cooking and baking and to do mending. Since she was a little girl these were things she had looked forward to doing when she became a wife.

Ephriam had one church meeting after another, counseling sessions, visiting the sick, catechism, baptism, marriages, funerals, church and community committee meetings, and frequently had to travel nearby to neighboring churches for meetings to support area charities.

There were plenty of meetings for Gretchen too. A young wife could learn a lot from the older women, and they were certainly anxious to teach her while respecting her as the pastor's wife. She never thought about all the things a young wife needed to learn and would be called upon to do. They seemed to never have time to themselves, but they recognized that was part of a pastor and his wife's life.

The congregation was overjoyed when Ephriam announced from the pulpit he and Gretchen were expecting their first child. Gretchen gave birth to a baby girl; they named her Mary.

It would be difficult for Gretchen to nurse Mary and maintain all of her other responsibilities. It was decided that rather than hire a nanny - Gretchen opposed that idea - they would hire a housekeeper to help with the household chores such as cooking, cleaning and doing the laundry. Gretchen could then concentrate on attending to Mary while meeting her responsibilities to the church and community.

Gretchen brought Mary to the church office in her fancy baby carriage. She had walked to the end of town eager to tell her husband that she had hired a housekeeper. Ephriam was surprised she found someone suitable so quickly; he would have liked to interview her before she was hired. But Gretchen told him that he would have absolutely no objections to her, for she was a perfect candidate. He wanted to know how Gretchen could be so sure. "She traveled from Philadelphia when my mother happened to mention to her employer, a friend of my family, that I was searching for a housekeeper who was efficient, dependable, and was qualified to help with the baby." The family friend sent her North to Hamlin with a letter of recommendation. The letter of recommendation was so complimentary Gretchen was convinced she had been blessed to find her. Ephriam finished his office work and pushed Mary's carriage while the young couple walked home, greeting and talking to people on the way.

"Wait here, I'll go get her." Ephriam waited anxiously, allowing his wife the pleasure of surprising him. Instead of surprise, it was a shocking experience; Gretchen's happiness was Ephriam's horror. Jeanie Belvoir walked into the parlor and greeted Ephriam! "I'm pleased to meet you sir!"

Ephriam was speechless. Hiding his shock from Gretchen, he faked a smile, and said quietly, "I'm sure you'll be happy here." She responded, "I'll be happy to help in any way I can." She glanced at Ephriam and said, "I'm especially excited about helping with Mary; she's such a lovely baby, I love holding her in my arms." Ephriam felt faint; his stomach became unsettled. He was revolted by the fact this despicable demon was holding his child, his and Gretchen's gift from God. He excused himself and retired to bed. He told Gretchen, "I don't feel the best, I feel very tired."

The next day he met Jeanie in the woods behind and across the field from the house. "I'm warning you, don't hurt my wife and daughter in any way." She put her face up against his. "Who do you think you are - warning me! I do the warning, you belong to me, or did you forget!" Showing his lack of respect for her made her very unhappy. She waved her left arm over her head and soon smoke could be seen coming from the woods. She had set the woods on fire! Ephriam turned and ran toward the center of town to alert the volunteer fire brigade. As he ran away he heard her screaming, "Do you think it's wise to threaten someone who can do what I have just done?"

She noticed his attitude had changed; he was a church and community leader, respected by his parishioners, married to a wonderful woman, a father to a lovely child; he no longer believed he needed to put up with her. He considered ignoring the warnings she gave him in Philadelphia.

He knew he couldn't get rid of her; Gretchen was happy with the way she performed her job, and she certainly wouldn't give up her mission; her purpose for being on Earth was to watch him. He was stuck with her. She was one of Satan's agents. She was surely a demon.

She had shown him her magical powers. It was her decision whether Mary lived or died. He took her threats to harm Anne very seriously. He searched the Book of Revelation

and found the passages that confirmed her story. He con-
ceded that no matter how happy and successful he ever became, he would have to deal with Jeanie Belvoir. Resisting
her, no matter how subtle, was only going to endanger him,
Gretchen, Mary, his parents, Anne, or anyone she believed
he cared about.

Reverend Herr had ignited his desire to do the research
necessary to find out exactly why he was saddled with this
lifetime burden and what part he is supposed to play in some
sort of plan that is evidently brewing up and hovering over
the town of Hamlin.

He strolled out into the back yard and found Jeanie in the
garden squatting while picking beans. Standing over her, he
asked, "Just what is the reason for your attachment to me?
We have shared many happy hours together, but why must
you now treat me so badly? I have done nothing to cause
the wrath of Satan except perhaps heal a few sick people."
She continued to pick beans and never looked up at him.
Looking down at her, he could see inside her simple cotton
dress, her small but supple breasts; they would tempt any
weak man. He couldn't help remembering being inside of
her. He walked to the edge of the grass and sat on the steps
leading from the porch and noticed that she wasn't wearing
any underwear. He wondered what she did when she had her
period. She glanced up at him, catching him staring at her
genitalia.

At times she could read his mind, and at that moment she
knew what he was thinking. "What purpose would be served
if I were to menstruate?" Ephriam wasn't prepared for the
question; the answers he was searching for didn't include
an explanation of Jeanie's biological make-up, if she in fact
had a biological make-up. He decided to ask anyway, "Are
you of the flesh?" She smiled, happy that she had spiked
his sexual curiosity. "Watch me piss!" She pointed to her
vagina, snapped her fingers and began urinating. Snapping

her fingers again, she stopped. Again she snapped her fingers and again she began urinating. "How is that for control!" To him it was fascinating.

She stood up; she looked inside the back door to make sure nobody would overhear her. "Anytime you want to fuck me just ask. You can have all you want anyway you want it. I'll do things to you Gretchen can't even imagine doing." He had to admit that she was a beautiful woman, she was sensual, short and petite, her chocolate brown skin was flawless. He was always taught that the man initiates sex. The sex with her was traumatic for him because she took the role of aggressor; it wasn't like that with Catherine and Gretchen. He had been gentle with them; they were willing, but he nevertheless had to seduce Catherine and marry Gretchen. Jeanie had aroused him more than he had ever been aroused before. With her it was a perfect sexual act; it was too perfect. Machine like and incapable of falling short in performance, she could turn a man's member into hard, smooth, polished granite because she's a demon.

That night he walked to the church and prayed at the altar. He always did this when he needed extra guidance and inspiration. He thanked God he knew who Jeanie Belvoir was and what she was up to. He was human, he was a man, he did find her attractive, her short dresses and sexual exhibitions did arouse him. He thanked God for giving him the strength to resist her evil temptation; evidently the Holy Spirit did have a stronger presence in him. He remembered Balair telling him that during his moments of honesty that horrible night in Harrisburg.

A few days later a man showed up late into the night, pounding on the Bernharter's big thick door. Dirty, ragged and exhausted, he explained that he and his family were wanderers passing through the area and were now camped in a small wagon near Franklinsburg. He had awakened an old woman who lived next to the church who told him

where the minister lived. "My daughter, who is unmarried, is with child and has gone into labor. She's in great
pain, and my wife sent me for help because it's going to
be a breech birth." He was speaking frantically. "I need
a midwife and a minister to pray for us. The baby will be
lost, and my daughter will die if someone doesn't help!"
Ephriam asked, "Where exactly is your wagon? There is a
doctor in Franklinsburg, you should have gone there!" The
man was irritated by this admonishment. "I have no time
for this, your village is as close to the main road as Franklinsburg. Pastor, I'm begging you, can you come and help
me?" Ephriam had begun to get dressed in the vestibule,
and now had wrapped his heavy coat around himself. "I'll
go to your wagon and pray for you and your family, but
I'll have to send you to Franklinsburg to get the doctor. A
breech baby needs to be delivered by a doctor."

Jeanie came out of her room putting on her robe. "I'll go
along, I can act as a midwife; I've delivered babies." Ephriam, not wanting Jeanie to be involved, responded, "No need
for you to come, we'll get the doctor." The man had a different reaction. "Yes! Please come along and help, there might
not be time to get the doctor!"

Ephriam quickly hitched up the horse to his buggy and
hurriedly followed the man down the road toward Franklinsburg. Halfway there, sitting back into the woods that lay
along the main road was the man's wagon.

They heard the young girl's screams as they approached.
Ephriam gave the man directions and told him to go get the
doctor. Jeanie yelled, "No need to get the doctor now, stay
here in case I need your help!" It was a horrid two hours
until Jeanie somehow got the infant out of the young girl.
Later everyone was resting quietly, exhausted physically and
emotionally. The man and his wife slept, and after nursing
the baby boy, the new mother and her child slept also.

Ephriam had built a fire, and now he and Jeanie sat there

on a fallen tree trunk, gazing into the flames while trying to stay warm. "While I was picking beans you asked me the key question, the question I chose not to answer then, but now perhaps is a proper time to explain certain things to you." Ephriam wasn't quite sure this was the proper time. He had been awoken from a sound sleep; it was dark, it was cold, and he wasn't in the mood for conversation.

"Ephriam, the miracle that you must warn me about is the second birth of Jesus Christ, the Second Coming of your Lord, who will cast Satan away and deliver the believers to God. If I allow that to happen I will perish too, because I am one of Satan's angels." She reminded him that everything she was describing is in the Bible. "It's all in the Book of Revelation, written in your scriptures. For me to survive I must follow my instructions." Ephriam knew better than to scoff at what most would consider preposterous. Since he had seen her at work, he knew her power. The most tragic, horrid, and scariest part for Ephriam was the fact that he was powerless to stop her from doing whatever she decided to do.

"Ephriam, you are one of God's invocators, which means that you could very well be the person who is charged with watching over the birth of the infant when it's time for the Second Coming." She stood up and glanced into the wagon, noting that everyone was still asleep. "The birth could take place anytime or anywhere, but wherever it takes place, an invocator must be there. You are one of many, perhaps thousands, and Satan is watching each one of you – he's going to resist all God's efforts to send the Savior to deliver His believers to Heaven."

Ephriam asked, "Well, maybe this baby could be the Lord. What then?" She had a quick answer in the form of advice. "Ephriam, worry about baby Mary, and the babies of church members, don't worry about the baby here. Go home and get some sleep. Tell Gretchen not to worry; I'll be home to cook breakfast and help with Mary."

She wasn't going to take any chances. She questioned why this man's wagon just happened to break down near Hamlin and Ephriam's house. Why did he come looking for Ephriam instead of a doctor? Was Ephriam needed in case the baby needed healing to survive? Would Ephriam immediately become the baby's guardian? Where was the baby's father? Could this baby be a result of a miracle, conceived by God? Ephriam was searching for answers to his questions, but some questions didn't have answers, at least not yet.

She waved to Ephriam as he drove off and then turned her attention to the family members still sleeping in the wagon. The two knives lying by the fire were convenient; she clutched one in each hand and crawled into the wagon. Jeanie became the beast; she heaved and growled, as her whole body became twisted and convulsive. Vomit spewed from her mouth, splashing up against the canvas covering the wagon. Her arms and legs became the same length while growing clawed feet and hands. Her face was so distorted it was unrecognizable as a human; her skin became scaly, she became a creature not unlike a small black dragon with feathers.

She began viciously stabbing the man and his wife; blood was splattering onto the inside of the canvas, on the sides and even to the top. There was no crying out, her knifing was so swift they didn't have time to react when they were awoken. Jeanie was covered with blood. She continued to use her awesome strength to stab the couple, perhaps twenty or twenty-five times before she finally paused. Using the back of her feathered claw to wipe the blood from her eyes, she now turned her attention to the daughter and her baby. The girl lay there frozen with terror. At first she hoped the vicious creature would be satisfied killing her parents; now she realized she was going to die. She was weak and tired, but she began to fight back, putting up fierce resistance. Jeanie wanted to get it all over with, so with ease she quickly slashed the girl's throat with one of the knives and drank some of her blood to satisfy her vile appetite. Then she killed the baby with one thrust of the other while he lay in his mother's arms.

Eating the infant ensured, if he was the Christ child, he would never rule and save mankind from evil. She dragged the three corpses from the wagon and strung them up using the wagon's rope; using yet more of her horrible and awesome force, she gutted their bodies like a hunter does to his catches.

Her stomach was full, unable to digest its contents; it felt like it was going to explode. She walked a short way to the small creek and vomited into the rapid flowing water. Exhausted, she collapsed and slept for an hour while her body returned to normal. She awoke to the normal pain she always had to endure while her muscles were retreating back into human form after being pulled, stretched and distorted. Covered with blood, by now coagulated and caked on her and her dress, she sat in the small stream and washed the blood from her hair, face, arms and legs. She washed her clothing, scrubbing hard to get the blood washed out, and then she walked the two miles home to Hamlin.

Because he was up most of the night, Ephriam slept later than usual. In the afternoon people began stopping at the house telling him of the butchered family. The sheriff stopped by to tell him he has no suspects but that the killers must've been very strong men. "It took a lot of might to gut those poor people, that's a hell of a way to die." He described that the bodies were hung from high tree limbs before they were disemboweled. "Their bloody insides were laying on the ground, blood dripping into three pools of blood on the ground. Ephriam asked, "What about the baby?" Ephriam's neighbor had told the sheriff about the man coming to her the night before asking for help with delivering his daughter's baby. "There ain't no baby nowhere; I'm thinking maybe that's why the family was killed - for the baby."

Ephriam knew better. Feeling sick, he excused himself and took a walk, falling to his knees as soon as he was
far enough into the woods. He needed to vomit, but unlike
Jeanie, he wasn't reacting to his stomach's contents. He was
vomiting for the same reason he did in Jeanie's bedroom. He
was reacting to more of the demon's vile behavior, behavior
that knows no boundaries, behavior that includes viciously
murdering innocent people.

He stood up and walked back to the house. Jeanie was
standing on the back porch. "Gretchen sent me to find you;
she wants to know if you are alright." He answered, "How
could I be alright? What did you do with that baby?" She
took a long pause, then finally answered, "It's best that you
not attend the birth of any babies, just in case they're boys."
He decried, "It's my job to minister to my parishioners, and
if that includes being there when a woman is giving birth,
then I must be there." Jeannie responded coldly, "You're the
pastor; you decide what you want to do; maybe I'll decide
to kill the baby boys as fast as God sends them. You know, I
can do that if I want."

He picked up a huge rock and hurled it toward her. She
easily dodged it, and it went through the window into the
kitchen. Doing that made her scream with anger. "Ephriam, don't try to hurt me, it'll make me angry, maybe angry
enough to wave my arm and kill Gretchen with fever, cripple
Mary, or send Anne to Hell!"

Gretchen called out, "What is a rock doing on the kitchen
floor? Who broke the window?" He walked into the house
and said, "I threw the stone. I threw it because I wanted to."

Then he told her that they would not be having any more
children.

Gretchen reacted like most women married to over-
worked men. She let it pass.

†

Chapter 15

1845

Ephriam takes a sabbatical

For over four years Ephriam had been working very long hours, most times from dawn to dusk, finding just enough time to have meals with Gretchen and Mary. He took just enough time for sleep to keep going, many nights it was interrupted by loud knocks on the door announcing a sudden death, a difficult pregnancy, or a serious injury, all requiring the pastor to be present to get the family through the crisis. Most times he would ride with them in their carriage and depend on them to bring him home when they felt it was time. If he could, he would quickly hitch up his own carriage, or more often saddle up one of his horses; they always seemed more resistant to the harness in the middle of the night. No matter what method of transportation was used, it was a bumpy, dark, and uncomfortable ride; it was worse on a bitter cold winter night or a hot, humid and rainy summer one.

Gretchen, although she was always a good pastor's wife, would occasionally sulk and ask, "Who will comfort us if a crisis came down upon this family?" Ephriam didn't take the time to ponder such hypothetical situations; he was aware of the strain his work put on Gretchen, but she knew as well as he did that a major part of his job was to share the grief and offer comfort to the congregation's families. Sickness, even fever, didn't excuse him from these awful nights when he was called out.

Very aware his job took time away from his family, he also realized his professional life lacked time to reflect, to pray, to read, and to discuss faith, theory, and other issues of the church with other clergy, especially the ones with many years of experience.

He thought perhaps a sabbatical could be arranged. He didn't like the idea of asking Bishop Benjamin Gruver for time off. Gruver was the man who ran the synod; he was the man who would assign a supply minister to St. Luke's if he approved Ephriam's request for a church sponsored sabbatical. Church sponsored sabbaticals gave pastors the opportunity to write and do research and earn their master's degree. All church sponsored sabbaticals had to be approved by Bishop Gruver. He didn't like the extra work processing the paperwork and then monitoring a pastor's sabbaticals. He rarely approved sabbaticals for young pastors. Ephriam figured he didn't have much chance getting approved. He decided to wait until the October synod conference, and then approach Gruver while he would be in a more hospitable mood.

Benjamin Gruver came from a privileged family; his wealthy landowner father made sure that he was installed at a church attended and supported by other wealthy landowners. When there was an opening to replace the retiring bishop of the northeastern synod, Gruver had plenty of influential people in his corner supporting his appointment. He was voted in overwhelmingly by the hundred or so pastors and lay leaders of the member congregations. He liked the job because he didn't have to prepare a weekly sermon, got to travel and visit member churches, be pampered and treated as an honored guest, and deliver his brief comments from the pulpit that he repeated verbatim at every church service he attended.

In August Ephriam got a letter from Reverend Doctor Frank Herr inviting him to Canada for a visit. Herr was now a senior fellow at the Christian Studies Institute, an ecumenical research center that embraced and encouraged clergy from all Christian denominations to search for common ground in the teaching of Christian dogma. It was the type of environment Herr yearned for after years of teaching at the seminary where the curriculum understandably and necessarily was in accordance with strict Lutheran doctrine. Frank Herr often told Ephriam that he was one of his all time favorite students. Ephriam somehow found that hard to believe, figuring it was just Herr's way of encouraging him to do his best. Ephriam always did excellent work, but after years and years of being a good student, compliments had eventually lost their luster. However, with this letter from Professor Herr in his hand, Ephriam began to think that maybe Herr was actually impressed by his scholarship.

Herr, now seventy-four years old, had been overdue to retire from the seminary. He finally moved to Canada to accept this position that provided him the time and resources to study ancient documents. Three archaeologists had discovered ancient scrolls in Mesopotamia and brought them back to the institute fifteen years earlier. They were written in Aramaic. The institute offered Herr the position to study the scrolls and translate the passages into English because he was an authority on the various languages used during Christ's time.

After reading the letter from his mentor, Ephriam reminded Gretchen, "No one can interpret the prophets' messages like Reverend Herr can; he brings their words alive; he invigorates their messages; he replenishes the faith in all of us." Gretchen was happy the professor wrote, she had known him in Philadelphia even before he had married her and Ephriam. She was well aware of the impact he had on her husband's life.

She had an idea. "Darling, why don't you write Reverend Herr and ask him if you can take a sabbatical at his institute? Perhaps you could lecture or serve as one of his assistants." Ephriam was delighted at her suggestion. He would be able to read, pray, and conference with Herr and the other distinguished professors; they all had doctorates in religion. "Gretchen, I could learn so much!"

Reality returned. "Gruver isn't going to approve a sabbatical for me." Gretchen watched her husband's high spirits turn to despair in a matter of seconds. "Of course he will! He might turn you down, but he doesn't have the courage to turn down Reverend Frank Herr!"

Ephriam quickly sent off a letter to Canada. Weeks past, three or four, and then a couple more went by. One day a letter from the Synod arrived granting him a sabbatical and appointment as an intern at Christian Studies Institute in Canada!

A letter arrived a few days later from Herr informing Ephriam that all accommodations had been made; the internship will be for three months. He was expected in two weeks; it wasn't very much notice!

Reverend Charles Hill arrived later in the week. He would serve St. Luke's while Ephriam was away. Gretchen prepared dinner for Hill and his wife and introduced them to James and Maggie Zimmerman who would be providing a studio apartment for the couple during their stay in Hamlin.

Later that night Ephriam and Gretchen talked. "I barely have enough time to brief Reverend Hill on all the things he needs to know before I leave." His face reflected all the weariness he felt. Gretchen responded, "Reverend Hill will do just fine, he'll find his way around, and everyone here will help him." She cut Ephriam short when he began to give her an argument. "Darling, he's a veteran pastor, do you believe you are the only one who can minister to our people?" Ephriam said, "Of course not!" Gretchen quickly followed up, "Then forget about this obsession with working day and night to 'brief' him, soon you'll be too exhausted to travel to Canada!"

After the long, tiresome train ride, Ephriam arrived at the institute; he was taken to Herr's home where they had a pleasant reunion. Herr had settled into a wonderful environment for an academic. The institute had given him an attractive house to live in, built in the Gothic style to match the institute's other buildings. The cozy house included a home office and a library to house his books and papers; both had hearty fires burning in their fireplaces to warm the wood paneled spacious rooms with their high ceilings. Herr had been assigned two Catholic nuns to serve as his staff. Sister Dominique was his personal assistant who took care of the household, greeted guests, managed his appointments, and supervised the married couple, Cuban immigrants, who worked as the domestic help. The man worked as the gardener and messenger; the wife cleaned the house, did the laundry, and cooked and served the meals.

Dominique was a member of the Dominican order, born and raised in Quebec twenty-four years earlier. She was short and petite with a pretty face; her short brown hair was hidden by her black and white habit that was closely fitted around her face and reached to the floor. English was her second language; she spoke it with a thick French accent. She had a pleasant way of dealing with people but did her job in a no nonsense manner. She was firm with Frank Herr, especially when it came to him following his schedule and meeting his daily commitments. She was devoted to the old man; he treated her so well she came to love him as a father.

Sister Josephine was his research assistant. Frank Herr had saved Josie Taylor's life. Before the young black girl took her vows and became Sister Josephine, she suffered being raised by an aunt in the slums of Philadelphia. The woman did only one good thing for Josie during all the years she had custody of her; she took her to mass and enrolled her in instruction.

She was slender and pretty, with a broad smile and a wonderful sense of humor, always anxious to help the less fortunate. Her mother, a heroin addict, didn't know who fathered the girl. She listened in school, attended mass every Sunday, and included prayer in her daily life, developing a deep religious faith and sense of spiritual growth.

She visited the Lutheran Seminary Chapel one Saturday afternoon, fascinated by it's beautiful limestone exterior. That day she met Reverend Herr, who had just performed a marriage ceremony. She was very chatty and articulate for an eleven-year-old; she asked him questions about the beautiful chapel and the music she overheard while standing outside during the wedding ceremony. She impressed him; he wanted to know more about her. He walked her home, met her aunt and began helping the woman and Josephine in many ways. He provided her with spiritual and practical guidance and spent hours helping her with her schoolwork. When she started high school she began assisting him with his research projects. She was very smart, adapted well to his work habits, sharing his good days, and tolerating him on days he was demanding, somber and impatient. He came to rely on her probably before she was old enough to accept the responsibilities. She accepted the challenges and kept improving each year they worked together. She had pleaded with her aunt to send her to parochial school; she flourished at St. Margaret's School, and then Central Catholic High School. After graduation she spent two years in a nearby convent as a novice, and after fulfilling her term, she took her vows of chastity and poverty and full inclusion in the convent. During the years she served at the convent she remained close to Frank Herr. He was like a father to her. Six years later, when

Herr decided to retire and work at the institute, Sister Josephine asked him if he would take her with him.

She was twenty-seven years old now; she was serious, focused, and dedicated to her work. She and Dominique lived very simply, with a group of twenty or so other nuns, in frugal quarters prescribed by the Church and provided by the institute just across campus, a quick five-minute walk from Herr's house. Each nun shared a small room with one other; there was a common parlor.

After dinner, Ephriam was taken to a guest cottage for a day or two of rest. He had read many of Herr's writings while attending his classes, and now he would have the opportunity to share some time with these old scrolls that the old man planned to study the rest of his life.

They quickly got to work. Ephriam was at first uneasy with this peer exchange, having thought provoking discussions instead of the formality of the lecture, with the man he admired more than any other. Ephriam's questions and Herr's answers always turned into lengthy conversations, sometimes continuing over the course of days.

There was never a lack of detail, nor did the old man ever doubt Ephriam's faith. Herr said, "While I pursue my research I question the writers of scripture to strengthen faith, not to find reason not to believe." His objective was always to dig deeper, find answers to questions that have gone unanswered for thousands of years. He said, "After spending my entire adult life studying scripture, I have never found any contradictions that I feel can't be explained logically."

Ephriam was sure that this wise elder was blessed with a talent to interpret and understand the word of God. Herr further explained, "Religious research has never scared me. I never believed I would ever uncover some ancient scroll someplace that would reveal that Jesus Christ was a hoax!"

Ephriam was anxious to confess his awful plight to the wise old man; he desperately wanted relief from the stress he had been enduring for such a long time. He knew Herr would believe the far-fetched assertions and keep the facts secret. Ephriam could finally tell someone not only about his healing powers, but also about Jeanie Belvoir and the affect she is having on his life. "She claims to be a demon; she told me I'm an 'invocator,' whatever that means." Ephriam failed to realize that he was putting Frank Herr's life in jeopardy by confessing his plight to him.

Ephriam felt more confident when he saw that Frank Herr's face lacked any hint of surprise or disbelief. "I'm going to read some ancient scrolls that we've been studying here at the institute. When I'm finished I'll send for you." Ephriam used the time for some much needed solitude. Being alone meant there was time for prayer and meditation and to visit the institute's vast library. He never doubted that the wise old man, the man he trusted completely, would find some answers.

Herr spent the next three days in isolation in the institute's archives reading some of the ancient scrolls. He interpreted some of the passages to prophesize that invocators, perhaps thousands of them, would be selected to watch over the Second Coming of Jesus Christ, to help usher in the full glory of the messianic age and the final judgment because it will be necessary that Christ himself returns to Earth in order to rule.

Herr became convinced that Christ would again come as an infant despite scripture proclaiming he would step down from the clouds. He found that the ancient scrolls did contradict slightly some passages in the books of the Bible. He was obsessed with studying the differences and deciphering these new revelations and prophesies.

He searched the Book of Revelation for signs that would reveal how Ephriam fit into the scheme of things. He wasn't disappointed.

"Then a great sign appeared in Heaven: there was a woman, whose dress was the sun and who had the moon un-

der her feet, and a crown of twelve stars on her head. She was soon to give birth, and the pains and suffering of childbirth made her cry out. Another sign appeared in Heaven. There was a huge red dragon with seven heads and ten horns, and a crown on each of his heads. With his tail he dragged a third of the stars out of the sky and threw them to earth. He stood in front of the woman who was about to give birth, in order to eat her child as soon as it was born. Then the woman gave birth to a son, who will rule over all nations with an iron rod. But the child was snatched away and taken to God and his throne. The woman fled to the desert; there God had prepared a place for her, where she will be taken care of for twelve hundred and sixty days. Then war broke out in Heaven! Michael and his angels fought against the dragon, who fought back with his angels; but the dragon was defeated, and he and his angels were not allowed to stay in Heaven any longer. The huge dragon was thrown out! He is that old serpent, named the Devil, or Satan, that deceived the whole world. He was thrown down to earth, and all his angels with him."

He sent for Ephriam. "I believe you might be a facilitator, or as this woman calls you, an invocator, for the Second Coming of Christ, who I believe is going to return again as an infant. I also believe this woman's claim that there are thousands of invocators presently alive on Earth. You might be one of the selected to play a major part in this Second Coming; then again when the time comes you might not even be alive anymore. The coming could happen tomorrow, it could happen a hundred years from now, two hundred years, three hundred years, even a thousand years. I'm pretty sure that as the invocators die, they are replaced." Ephriam seemed even more confused now. "Listen Ephriam, God is a mysterious God, you mustn't try to understand the passage of time, because it is God's great secret. His seven days could be a billion years to us."

Jeanie's warnings contained much of the same information. Ephriam was anxious to hear more. "Ephriam, at first I
thought maybe the scrolls are talking about something else.
We have been challenged here at the institute by contradict-
ing interpretations. But the Book of Revelation, I think, re-
veals and identifies Jeanie, and because of that, her claiming
that you are an invocator seems to have credibility. She's
been assigned to you because Satan doesn't know when,
where, or which invocators will be involved."

Herr stressed that if Ephriam's role turns out to be significant, "Jeanie will kill Gretchen, Mary, Anne, and other
members of your family unless you abandon God and his
plan for you. Ephriam asked, "How can she be stopped?"
With a weary look, Herr replied, "I don't know if she can
be stopped." That statement stunned Ephriam. "Evidently
you have been put in the middle of a very dangerous situation, a tug of war. At any moment something terrible could
go wrong; fire could consume Earth in a matter of hours.
The agnostics ignore the seriousness of it, and the atheists
laugh at the prospect, but I know things are not going the
way they are supposed to be, and that puts everything in
jeopardy."

Herr's statement, *"I know things are not going the way
they are supposed to be"* was fixed into Ephriam's mind;
that was the statement that got him scared.

Frank Herr had great hope for mankind. "Ephriam, you
possess the Holy Spirit in such a profound way that allows
you to heal the sick. You are without original sin, and you
can rid a person of original sin." As an ordained minister
Ephriam felt the awesome impact of this particular Herr revelation. "I suspect it is because you have been selected an
invocator. As clergy, you baptize and save the sinner from
Hell. But even more than that, you have the special power
to use the Holy Spirit to drive Satan's spirit from those possessed by it. But remember, you can't rid someone of origi-

nal sin unless Satan's spirit is inside them; they must be possessed. Those are the rules."

Walking back to his quarters Ephriam thought about another Herr revelation; *"Those are the rules."* Ephriam wanted to know who in Heaven or Hell makes the rules!

Chapter 16

1845

Jeanie goes to Canada

Now that Mary was older, Gretchen again was faced with all the social demands that are part of the life of every pastor's wife. She felt completely comfortable with Jeanie, a perfect caregiver, taking care of the baby, housecleaning, laundry, and her invaluable help in the kitchen. Since Gretchen's heavy involvement in the church and community's social life required a lot of entertaining, cooking for luncheon and dinner guests, baking for meetings, plus contributions to the church suppers, bake sales, bazaars and the many other activities, she was pleased with Jeanie's willingness to assist her. She met the demands easily, the more responsibility Gretchen gave her, the more she seemed to flourish.

She would be quiet and respectful, assuming the role of servant except when alone with Ephriam. She asked Gretchen, "When is Reverend Bernharter's sabbatical ending?" Gretchen appreciated Jeanie's interest. "Our man of the house will be home in three weeks. I'm sure many of our parishioners are anxious to have him back in the pulpit; Reverend Hill is a good pastor, but he doesn't know our congregation. When Ephriam preaches, he seems to preach to each of us personally because he knows each of us." Jeanie agreed. "People depend on him. He accepts their problems as his own, and it's good that he's getting much needed rest. He needs to relax and not work." She was curious why he elected to go to Canada, instead of the seashore, or spending time in New York City, indulging in big city culture.

Gretchen explained. "He's spending his time up there with Reverend Frank Herr, who taught at seminary and retired to do research at the institute up there. He is a Biblical scholar, and Reverend Bernharter wanted to discuss prophesy with him and to get answers to questions that have been troubling him." Hearing this did not make Jeanie happy. She remembered Frank Herr. Ephriam had told her much about him, in particular how knowledgeable and perceptive he is about the history of religion. She realized she made a mistake allowing Ephriam to get away from her, out of her sight. She was angry with him for not telling her he was going to be spending his sabbatical with Herr. She knew being inspired by Frank Herr while researching prophesy, reading scripture, and studying historical documents could give Ephriam knowledge about the future that she preferred him not to know.

Two days later Jeanie told Gretchen, "I need to go home to Philadelphia for a few days, I just got a letter from my sister. She told me our mother is dying, and I should come quickly and spend a few days with her before she passes away." Gretchen was naturally concerned and sympathetic; she advanced Jeanie train fare and spending money.

Instead, Jeanie took the train to the institute, leaving late into the evening, traveling all night, and then at daybreak enduring eight more hours of jarring and bouncing over the rails, arriving late into the night. It was a frigid, still night; she took a carriage to the institute, its wheels cracking the ice while snow swirled all about the horse's legs. When she got there she entered the reception hall and announced to the security guard, "Hello, my name is Mademoiselle Belvoir. I am to report to Reverend Herr's home, I'm his new house-keeper." The security guard was very helpful; he carried her bags, and because of the lateness of the night, escorted her the two blocks to Herr's house. She stopped him short at the sidewalk that led to Herr's front door. "Thank you for your help, I'll be fine now." He tipped his cap and disappeared around the corner, returning to his post at the reception hall. Jeanie didn't knock on the front door or enter through the front door. Instead, she walked along the dark and narrow walkway leading to the lush garden and back porch, twisting and turning to get past the bushes scraping against her and then pushing away the ferns slapping her in the face; she finally got to the back of the house.

Audaciously, she turned the doorknob to the unlocked door and entered the kitchen. Adrenaline wasn't flowing through her veins, her heart wasn't beating rapidly; Satan had not given her this human dynamic, among others, as needed tools to function naturally on Earth. She had no fear of being caught by the police, being arrested as a burglar, or having to explain why Reverend Bernharter's housekeeper would travel to the institute to break into Reverend Herr's house. Her only fear was Satan's terrible wrath if she failed to carry out her mission.

She found Frank Herr in front of the fire in his study. The peaceful and contented look on his face while asleep on the thick and comfortable leather couch was compatible to his casual grace while awake, the persona of a saved man, a man so assured of his destiny with his Savior in Heaven.

She became the beast, heaving and growling and evolving into the grotesque dragon exhaling that blue smoke. Twisting and convulsing, the vomit she spewed all over him awakened the man. With her overpowering strength she twisted his neck so forcefully that he was dead in an instant. She crushed his skull with one forceful blow and ripped it off, tossing it to the floor. Gripping the bottom of his rib cage with both her hairy, clawed hands, she tore it open and ripped out his heart; she threw it across the room while it was still beating. She pulled out his insides, took bites of it and drank the dripping blood, then threw each handful into the firewood bucket. Her frantic slinging caused some of the bloody slop to dangle over the edges. She ripped off his arms, tossing them into the air. The peaceful richly furnished cottage was turned into a living hell. Hogs being slaughtered are given more dignity than what this man of God got. The most evil and contemptible force destroyed Frank Herr, killed his brain and all that vast intelligence; wasted his heart and insides. She destroyed this brilliant and kind man with ferocious evil force.

He lay dead on the floor. Blood was splattered all across the white plaster walls, blood made the hardwood floor slippery; it was difficult to stand up. She hobbled into the dining room and lay on the floor. It took about an hour for her to turn back into a petite, ninety-five pound girl. Still not fully recovered from her aching muscles, stretched skin, and twisted spine, bones, and joints, she struggled to search his papers to discover his sources and to read his findings. She didn't notice a small piece of paper and pencil lying on the floor next to the couch, a note scrawled just before he dozed off.

Hours passed; now the sun was rising. She concluded from perusing his notes that what he had written was mostly hypothesis, conjecture, and speculation until just a few days earlier, but now he was on the verge of discovering the terrifying war of good versus evil that was presently taking place, and what role Ephriam was going to play as the future unfolded. She was not going to let Ephriam know about any of this.

Sister Josephine showed up for work and discovered the horrible scene. She became hysterical, falling to the floor and screaming loudly. His mutilated body was a pile of bloody flesh. His crushed skull lay across the room, his arms were lying next to his chair, and someone with overpowering strength ripped his chest open. Still on her hands and knees; her head was swaying as she wept. Then she noticed a clump of bloody matter. Crawling to get closer, her worst fears were realized, it was her beloved mentor's heart; his good heart had been torn from a caring and compassionate man and was tossed to the corner of the room to die a separate death. She thought, of all people, Reverend Herr should not have died without a heart.

She tore off a piece of her blood soaked habit and wrapped the heart in it, setting it down near his body. Then she placed his severed arms across his empty chest.

When the house servants arrived for work they discovered Josephine laying across his bloody body, crying uncontrollably, still hysterical. The husband ran to the institute's security office. The police were summoned.

Ephriam showed up just as they were taking Herr's body away. He was devastated; he tried to quiet Josephine and did his best to comfort her. The police arrived and began to examine the room. He knew a lot more than the police would ever know. He finally managed to calm Josephine down; she was still shaking when he sat her in a chair and gave her a glass of wine. She went upstairs and changed into the clean habit she kept at the house. They both sat in the dining room while the police continued to do their work. He wanted to give her more time, but he needed to ask her some questions before the police did. "Look around, see if you notice anything missing, anything out of place. It might be important." She got up from the chair; with his help they began slowly walking into the study; all the blood had dried by now.

"Don't touch anything!" The command came from a short fat detective with greasy wavy hair and large bushy sideburns. His voice startled Josephine. "Sister, I have a job to do here, I need to keep the room exactly as it is." Ephriam told him that Sister Josephine was Herr's assistant. "I'll be asking her some questions. Who are you?" Before he could answer the detective was called outside by one of the other officers. Ephriam took that opportunity to talk quickly to Josephine. "If you notice anything, tell me first." Josephine didn't really need to be told that. She also knew more than the police suspected. While staring at the floor she pointed to the torn piece of paper and a pencil lying on the floor next to the couch. Just then the detective came back inside. Josephine walked over to the couch and put her shoe over the note, her long habit also covering it. He confessed, striking a match on the window sill and lighting his cigar stub, "I never seen a murder like this, it's like a female lion ripping apart her prey in Africa did this, for Christ's sake." Ephriam knew who killed Frank Herr, and he also knew if he told the detective, Anne would be dead before sunset, and maybe Gretchen and Mary as well. And what about Josephine? What about Dominique? The detective barked, "Reverend, who did this? Tell me so I can get this monster, this son-of-a-bitch locked up before he does this to somebody else." Ephriam lied. "I have no idea officer, I have no idea. Reverend Herr had no enemies."

Later, after they were told they could leave, Josephine quickly picked up the note and crumbled it in her hand without looking at it, and then whisked past Herr's desk. Without any hesitation she grabbed the handle and picked up his thick leather bag. She played the role very well - carrying the bag confidently past the detective and out the door as if it belonged to her, always with her when she worked. As they left, the officer reminded them they would be called to police headquarters for questioning and to give statements. A more perceptive homicide detective would have noticed the gold embossed letters "FLH" on the bag.

They walked for about a block before she handed the

note to Ephriam. It was barely legible; it was obvious Herr had torn it from his notebook and scribbled the message while he was half asleep. It read "The + is hol."

He asked her, "Do you know what this means?" Josephine said no. He went back to his cottage to be alone and deal with the loss of a person he idolized. She had given him the leather bag; inside it were over a thousand pages of notes, all the notes he had taken during his research while at the institute. For now all he could think about was losing the man he idolized, and wondering how he was going to deal with his life's problems without the old wise man to help him. He prayed and meditated, and then tried to sleep.

†

Chapter 17

1845

Rosa comes to the door

A few hours later he awoke to the frantic knocking sound on his door. He assumed it was Josephine wanting to pray with him. Instead, a weeping young woman, shivering while holding an infant, stood in the cold dark night, driving sleet pelting her face, freezing rain encrusting her long, black braided hair and the shawl that was wrapped tightly around the child. She was an attractive woman with Italian features and accent. She pleaded, "My baby girl is sick, she's burning with fever." Ephriam was confused. "Woman, why are you bringing your child to me? I'm not a doctor." She was worn down, worried sick about her daughter. Holding the infant close to her bosom, she pleaded, "I've had the baby with the doctor. I need Reverend Herr to pray for her, but I heard something terrible has happened to him." Ephriam asked, "Did Reverend Herr pray for your child before?" She told him, "He prayed for my whole family. They told me yesterday you were a close friend of his and that you would pray for my baby." She wasn't going to take no for an answer. "Reverend, you will be rewarded for your acts of mercy."

Ephriam was very tired, but he invited her in and took

the baby from her. He held the infant for about ten minutes, putting his open hand on her head and praying for her. His heart raced, his breathing became labored. When he went to sit down on the settee, his reactions startled the mother. "Reverend, are you alright? Are you having difficulty breathing?" Ephriam, still holding the baby, put his head on the back of the settee. "I will be fine. Your baby is not seriously ill; she has fluid in her lungs, so she needs to be kept warm and given hot tea and other liquids." He knew that without his prayers the baby was surely going to develop pneumonia. He wondered how competent the doctor was, and how concerned he was about that possibility. Ephriam's healing power cleared the baby's lungs and broke her fever. Holding her in his arms saved her life.

"I do need to sleep some more, this has been a very tragic day for me." She stood up and thanked him for his prayers, unaware that his were far more powerful than Frank Herr's. She took the baby from his arms, and when she turned to leave she noticed the wrinkled piece of paper lying on the table with "The + is hol" scrawled on it. Horrified, she fell back into the rocking chair and began shaking uncontrollably; Ephriam thought she was having a seizure. He reacted by taking the baby from her. She yelled, " The cross is hollow! Why would Reverend Herr write such a thing? Maybe he's hidden something in it. Did you kill him?" Ephriam said, "I didn't kill him, I loved that man, just as you obviously did!" He tried his best to keep her calm. "How do you know his note means that the cross is hollow? It could mean it's holy." She jumped from the rocking chair and grabbed the note, tossing it into the fire. Starting to shake again, she countered, "Reverend Herr would never feel it necessary to tell us the cross is holy!" Ephriam, still very tired and was now confused. He didn't know who to trust. He wondered if this woman was sent by someone to help him or perhaps to harm him. Suddenly she fainted and fell onto the couch.

With his hands still full from holding the baby, he ran to the pantry to get her a glass of water. When he returned to the parlor she had regained consciousness. "What is your name, and who sent you here?" She stared at him with a confused look on her attractive face. "My name is Rosa, and nobody sent me. I just came." Ephriam was convinced she had been sent to him, but he suspected she didn't realize it. He was beginning to think like Frank Herr. He became convinced her purpose for coming to him was to make sure the note was thrown into the fire; then it occurred to him there could possibly be horrible consequences if Jeanie knew about the note.

He was sure Rosa was in danger now because she came to his quarters. Since she and her baby were at risk anyway, he didn't hesitate to ask her to help him search for the cross that might be hollow. Rosa offered to take the baby to her mother. "No, I don't want you to do that. It will be better if some of the nuns that Josephine and Dominique live with take care of her. I don't want to scare you, but I think you and your baby are in danger." He thought to himself; just being in his presence meant that if the baby was a boy, Rosa and the infant would already be dead.

They hurried to Dominique's room and told her to follow and then gave the baby to some of the other nuns to care for; they found Sister Josephine in bed from exhaustion. To avoid arrest for trespassing, Ephriam knew people who worked at the institute needed to accompany him and Rosa. "We think we have an important clue concerning the note." Hearing that, Josephine managed to find enough strength to go with them and help with the search.

He reminded Rosa, "There are probably hundreds of crosses here at the institute." She said, "I think Reverend Herr's favorite cross would likely be the hollow one." Ephriam appreciated how valuable her help had quickly become; if he was to finally submit to his life's awful circumstances and admit he had a problem, then it was easy for him to have faith that this woman, brought to him on this cold and foul weather night, would be unconsciously guided to lead him to the right cross.

While the four walked through the snow to the main chapel, the wind blowing away the last remnants of the stinging sleet, he thought again about his awful circumstance, overwhelmed with doubt and fear, being forced to live through an adventure with unknown variables that are evidently incomprehensible to most. What was going to happen next? What if all the prophecy is wrong? What if Satan decides to no longer tolerate the presence of these invocators? What if he becomes so desperate he uses his power, if he in fact has that power, to hurl all existence into a fiery ball of fire in an instant?

Being away from Gretchen gave him time to think of Jeanie. How could she be such a good friend and then turn into a vicious and ruthless Satanic murderer? He was inside her and in retrospect he couldn't deny that he enjoyed it after recovering from the initial shock of being assaulted. He could have loved her. He would have gone with her to some far away place where interracial marriage was tolerated. His sin was wishing she were mortal, not a murderer, not a demon, but a woman he could lay with and have children with. She was his ultimate temptation, tempting him to give up everything for her was her duty; she could then deliver him to Satan. His resounding faith in God is what saved him. His profound love for Gretchen saved him. Frank Herr saved him.

He asked, "Where is his favorite cross?" Rosa replied, "Oh, there's no question it's the large one in the cathedral's main sanctuary." Ephriam saw a problem. "That cross is over eight feet tall!" He felt helpless to get to it, but she again proved her worth. "There's a large ladder in the room behind the altar. It's the ladder they use to clean the chandeliers and the cross." He asked, "Do you think we could use it without someone seeing us?" She shrugged her shoulders. "Why are you afraid of being seen?" He told her he didn't want the police to see him, for he was sure they wanted to implicate him in the murder. He couldn't tell her the real reason for his worry; the thought of Jeanie finding out about religious secrets stuffed into a hidden compartment of a wooden cross terrorized him. Sister Josephine noticed he was fidgety and nervous. "Don't be scared. God is watching us right now." Her assurances didn't help ease his fears. He knew Jeanie would destroy anybody who read Frank Herr's prophecy about the Second Coming.

Sometime after midnight Ephriam climbed the ladder and took down the cross. After they laid the huge wooden piece along the tops of the pews, he began a thorough inspection while nervously looking over his shoulder for any sign of Jeanie; the three women were unaware of the real danger they were being exposed to.

He examined closely the carved raised sign of the trinity that was in the center of the cross, trying to move it left to right. He finally used his pocketknife to lift it up. Inside the compartment, measuring only about four inches wide, was a folded piece of thick paper. It was undated, but looked freshly written in ink, possibly to leave a secret record of a recent discovery, related to Ephriam's plight; the subject of their long conversations since their reunion. Herr wrote simply, *"Know the links and save them to seven of the 21st, then rattle, then conception."*

He experienced an eerie feeling; he knew it was prophesy as soon as he read it. Shaking, he walked outside and tore the note in half. Unnoticed by the three women, he put the worded portion in his pocket and asked Josephine for a candle. He burned the blank piece of paper in front of them.

All three of the women were curious. Rosa asked, "What does the note say? Is the future predicted?" Ephriam was sure he was saving their lives by being the only person to read the note. "No, there are no predictions. The note simply said he hoped someday all men would live in peace."

Burning what they thought was the note protected everyone from Jeanie. He didn't want to panic the nuns or Rosa, but he knew they were in danger, especially if Jeanie were still on campus. She might decide that the nuns should be destroyed because Herr confided in them, and they refused to reveal anything he shared with them.

Ephriam wasn't sure what Herr's note meant, but he realized it could be "the message" from God telling him he was the invocator selected.

He didn't need to be reminded that Jeanie, with Balair's help, would continue to hold Anne's soul as ransom.

He had a proposal for the nuns and was surprised they agreed to it. "I want both of you to come home with me; I can protect you. You're in danger here; I know who did this horrible thing to Reverend Herr, and I know why." Ephriam reasoned that as long as the nuns were close by, he could watch them; they would be spared if they were living in Hamlin.

Josephine said, "We will go with you because we know there is warm water in Hamlin." The next morning the three of them said goodbye to Rosa and then they hurried to the police station. They wrote out statements and promised they would return when the murderer was caught. Ephriam knew that was never going to happen.

The detective gave them more news. "These Spaniards that worked for the Reverend, where were they from?" Dominique answered, "They're Cuban, they came to us from Cuba." Taking a long drag from his thick cigar, he announced, "They're dead. I'm assuming the same killer, or killers, didn't want to take any chances they knew anything." Ephriam asked, "How were they murdered?" Plopping down in his chair, the weary officer said, "I've never seen anyone butchered like Reverend Herr and this couple. It would have taken two people to do what was done to this man and woman. Were they married?" He had this bad habit of asking a question and not waiting for an answer. "They were sexually abused, disemboweled, mutilated and chopped up into small pieces; whoever did this had a lot of rage built up inside and enjoyed killing people." Dominique asked, "How did you discover the bodies?" "The neighbors noticed the vultures and dogs dragging off the pieces." Being told that made her ill. The officer called out to his secretary for a glass of water. Josephine took Dominique outside for some fresh air.

Ephriam knew no human being, no matter how evil, could kill like this. Jeanie, the demon, did her job well.

Chapter 18

1846

Ephriam ministers to his congregation

Ephriam brought Frank Herr's briefcase containing all of his notes home with him. He was sure the institute's board of trustees would claim they were property of the institute. He knew they were probably right. However, he was sure they contained information that would be helpful dealing with the struggle he had been living with for all these years. He decided he was going to read every page of the notes. Unfortunately he never did.

The nuns were guests in Ephriam and Gretchen's home for a few weeks while they searched for a place to live. Jeanie was kind to them and helped Gretchen with the extra work involved having two house guests. The small Catholic Church in Franklinsburg met with them and asked if they would help establish a school. With the bishop's consent, they began recruiting children and seeking donations of books and pencils and paper. Soon they had fifteen Catholic children from nearby towns enrolled.

The nuns walked to the lake almost every day. They told Ephriam how beautiful they thought it was, and how much at peace they felt when they were near it. When he heard that one of his parishioners was going to sell her cottage he helped the Catholic Church arrange a mortgage with the bank in Jenkinstown to purchase the house for the nun's residence.

There was an outpouring of support from the community. Catholics, Baptists, Brethren, and the Lutheran members of St. Luke's helped the two nuns. Money was raised for a horse and carriage, furniture for their cottage, and donations of firewood and coal to keep them warm. The small amount of tuition the parents paid provided Josephine and Dominique with food and other necessities. They seemed very happy.

Ephriam visited often. "I worry about both of you, out here in the country is not a place for two nuns to be living, away from the security that the convent provides." Josephine took note of the insinuation. "My, my, Reverend Bernharter. Is it your opinion that we are two nuns lost in the wilderness?" Ephriam knew she was teasing, but he responded with seriousness. "I can't help but be concerned; there are things that exist in my life that make me very cautious, things I can't talk about to anyone." Dominique answered, "Oh, we're sure of that. But we're here because God has brought us here. This is a place of peace, this is a refuge." Josephine added, "We are supposed to be living next to Lake Stamen. So please be concerned for us, offer us aid whenever you can; we appreciate that, but don't fear for us, the Lord has put us here and will protect us here."

Now that his sabbatical was cut short, coming home to Hamlin meant a return to the long hours and hard work involved with being a country pastor. Soon he was assigned additional duties by the synod supplying small new congregations that had not yet found their own pastors. Grandfather Bernharter had been doing that for many years; his age was forcing him to slow down, and he found it increasingly more difficult to arise before the Sunday sun and take a one or two hour carriage ride to a tiny church tucked away in some valley and deep wooded primitive village. Many times the church had not been built yet; services were held outdoors until the cold weather, or rain, or snow, made it impossible. Under those conditions the small congregation would huddle inside a member's small house, standing so close they didn't have enough space to open their Bibles. The elder Bernharter would ask established congregations to donate a hymnal or two, and once he had a dozen he would take them along to the new beginner group. They would respond with hearty singing; that was his inspiration. Now his grandson was called to serve these pioneers up in the mountains and down in the valleys. Ephriam enjoyed preaching, even though his body and spirit constantly reminded him it was such hard work.

Simon Spatz, a wealthy farmer and wheelwright, donated land to build a church in Five Points, a small village about fifteen miles away. Ephriam married Reuben Delp, a young blacksmith, and pretty Magdalena Noll in the brand new sanctuary the following year. Magdalena was a distant relative of schoolteacher Hilda Noll. In 1876 he baptized their son Henry Adam Delp, and eventually baptized, confirmed married all of their children, as he did for so many other families. He gave the eulogies at the funerals of many. Allen Shalter gave land for another church, about ten miles further away from Spatz's, and when Reuben Delp and his brother Bennethum decided to found a new congregation, they asked Ephriam to be the pastor. He dedicated that church in a special Sunday worship service, just as he did at Spatz's. He had become a circuit preacher; serving these outlying chapels at the same time he was performing the duties of full-time pastor at St. Luke's.

He needed to stay busy; it helped him cope with Jeanie. He had a wonderful marriage to Gretchen, and together they raised Mary, a brilliant student, and like her Aunt Anne, a love of music, but with exceptional talent to match. By age seven she had become an accomplished pianist, giving concerts at many of the churches in the area. Mary took private lessons, but her exceptional talent yearned for the best formal training. When she was eleven years old Ephriam and Gretchen enrolled her in the Academy of Music in Philadelphia to receive her music and grammar school education. Anne had also studied there.

For the first time Ephriam felt Mary was safe; she was away from Jeanie. Gretchen, unaware of the danger imposed by Jeanie, wanted her to move back to Philadelphia as Mary's guardian.

"I'll feel much safer knowing Jeanie is with her." Ephriam took a firm stand against that idea. "Jeanie belongs here helping you. Mary will be taken care of by house parents."

Ephriam was having good feelings about his life. He was working hard helping people find God. Helping to start new congregations was especially rewarding. Mary seemed to flourish while studying music, and Gretchen was happy and fulfilled as a pastor's wife.

Watching out for Anne's well being was another matter. It was just a matter of time before Luther Bernharter came to see his grandson with bad news about the girl. "Your sister is in serious trouble, but she doesn't realize it. Your father has told me things that are very troubling to him and to me also."

Anne was twenty-six years old now. She was restless and she didn't show any interest in marriage or motherhood. She needed to find direction in her life. She had never been a good student and had resisted discipline during her teen years.

Because of what happened in Harrisburg, Ephriam knew that Anne needed to be watched closely. He had felt guilty not spending more time with her. He wished he could tell his father and grandfather the reason dear Anne behaved the way she did. "I know Anne has been a problem child, but I'm not aware of any serious trouble she is in."

Luther explained, "You know... me, your parents, and certainly you and your family, we are all looked up to in this community. Your sister's behavior is putting our family's standing in jeopardy, and you are going to have to stop her; she'll ruin our reputations!" Ephriam said, "I'll have a talk with her, grandpa." The old man shouted, "You better believe you'll have a talk with her!"

Ephriam had heard about the wrath his grandfather could muster. While growing up he contended with his firm demeanor and treatment; this was the first time he withstood one of his legendary outbursts.

Anne Bernharter was more than just a beautiful young woman. She lit a fire inside men. They were attracted to her beauty that was almost breathtaking. He was reminded of the reasons; her long blond, almost white hair flowed around her beautiful baby face with clear violet eyes and sensuous lips. Her alabaster complexion covered her flawless facial features and perfectly proportioned petite body.

Anne knew she was beautiful. Her personality had developed into one of snobbery. She would socialize with very few boys; she gave them the uncomfortable feeling they weren't worthy to be her escort. She seemed to enjoy rejecting them. Henry and Sally didn't discourage this behavior; they were sure being escorted by farmer's boys would keep her from studying music and painting in Philadelphia. With Stanton family help, meeting wealthy patrons of the arts would surely introduce her to the sons of wealthy prominent Main-Line businessmen.

Anne had learned to frustrate those around her using a technique of soft-speak. Those she offended, subtly or otherwise, could vent their displeasure with her in any number of ways; however they would only be faced with a quiet, composed and unemotional Anne.

Knowing Anne was always a second from death and delivery to Hell, Ephriam invited her to

meet with him at his church office. She had been reluctant at first, but then suddenly changed her mind, becoming almost excited with the prospect. They always greeted each other with an embrace and kisses on the cheek. "This has to be very important for my brother to meet with me at the church and not in his parlor." Ephriam got right to the point. "Mother and father went to grandpa and told them about a serious problem they are having with you." Her smile turned into a cold stare. He continued, "He didn't tell me what the problem is, and I've not asked mother and father." He was being firm and pastoral, not portraying the loving and protective brother. "Don't be silent with me, don't try to elevate yourself above me like you do with other people. I'm your minister, but remember I'm also your brother. I expect you to communicate with me, and I expect cooperation. I want to know what you are doing that is so troubling to the family." Anne decided to be gracious. "Dear brother Ephriam, I've been associating myself with people mother, father, and grandpa, find offensive - people who are fighters, warriors, people who have lost patience with the government's support of slavery, people who will break the law while helping the black man escape from the evil that exists in the South - they're radicals, they're Abolitionists. Ephriam, I'm one of them, I'm an Abolitionist!"

He was surprised. He never thought she had any political opinions, certainly not strong political commitment and passion for social issues that are needed to be a committed Abolitionist. "I must admit Anne, I'm impressed that you have become part of such a noble cause." Anne smiled and shook her head. "You have no idea what saving a run away slave entails." Typical of a radical, she had been using arrogance to shield herself from outsiders questioning her beliefs. "Evidently grandpa is a supporter of slavery, why else would he object to my involvement in this cause?" Ephriam knew the old man had preached against slavery for years, and he believed he was sincere. "Grandpa never in his life preached anything he didn't personally believe in. Maybe he just objects to you taking time away from your social life, your music, your painting, to pursue this cause." She stared at him coldly; he could see she was all prepared for confrontation. "Maybe this abolitionist movement, and the type of people who are involved in it, isn't something you should be involved in." She got up to leave. "You aren't saying the right things Ephriam. Don't get me riled up." He quickly said, "Please don't leave, stay and we'll talk some more about it. I will try my best to understand. Convince me this is what you need to do to have purpose in your life."

She finally confessed the real problem. "Grandpa doesn't object to the mission, not even my involvement with it. He became quite concerned only after mother and father told him that I am in love with a man who has broken laws and committed acts of violence and that I intend to go off with him. He has run away to Canada." Ephriam asked, "What crimes has he committed?" She held her head down to avoid eye contact. "He shot those two Virginia bounty hunters who came a couple of weeks ago to take back Old Black Joe, the hermit who lives up in the North Mountain. I'm sure you heard that two bodies were discovered last week."

He wanted to know all about this radical; she wasn't accustomed to revealing his identity but knew now was not the time to hold anything back. "His name is Robert Krieg; he has been an Abolitionist for a long time. He was born and raised in Switzerland; he has traveled the world. He believes no man should own another."

Ephriam was trying his best to be sympathetic. "If he killed two men he should face justice, stand trial. If he was justified he will be found not-guilty." Anne spoke up, "He and his fellows have robbed banks in Virginia, they've stolen slaves right out of the fields, they have beaten overseers." Her elucidation gave no doubt she was committed to this diehard. "Do you actually believe he would be found not guilty?" He knew she wasn't going to give him time to answer. "They'll hang him in Virginia if they don't hang him here."

She revealed details to him she dared not tell anybody else. "We're going to Montana and live just a few miles South of the Canadian border. There I will have babies and, in the darkness of night, help Robert and the fellows sneak runaways across the border."

Ephriam said, "Anne, I can't help a murderer, but I'll help you, whatever I need to do." She responded loudly, "Robert is not a murderer! You can help me by wishing me well, by saying nothing of this to mother and father, to grandpa, or to anybody else, until I'm gone."

He had read about the passionate dedication of Abolitionists. "I never suspected you would join a political cause." She got fiery again. "Political cause! Is that what you call it? You are a man of God; you know slavery is evil! It's a sin. It's against God!" He said, "I don't mean to sound callous; I'm against slavery, as you are." She slouched back into the chair and sighed.

He used his professional training to hide his worry. He wasn't worried about her gritty goals; he was worried because she was possessed. He was worried because he no longer would be able to watch and safeguard her. He needed to rid her of Satan before she went far away. He had no idea how to do it. If he failed, he would somehow need to keep her here even if that meant turning in Krieg. "I would like to meet this Robert Krieg; I want him to convince me he's devoted to you." A broad smile sallied across her beautiful face.

He wondered if Jeanie would allow Anne to leave. He hoped she wouldn't object. Wasn't Montana Territory just a blink of the eye away?

Josephine visited him at his office the next day. She seemed to sense when he was having problems. "You look more troubled than usual." A letter to Frank Herr would help solve this one, but his guidance was lost forever. Sister Josephine would have to do. "My sister has joined the Abolitionist Movement; she is unmarried and planning to move to Montana to smuggle Negroes into Canada. I can't let her go with part of Satan's evil spirit dwelling inside her."

"I know what Balair did to Anne, and I also know you have the power to heal her. Reverend Herr discovered while reading the ancient scrolls that any person who is able to heal the sick, as you can, is without original sin and has the power to exorcise Satan from a possessed person."

Suddenly Ephriam remembered that Herr had told him he could replace original sin with the Holy Spirit, but only if Satan already possessed the person. Josephine said, "If you exorcise Satan from Anne you will protect her from him. You won't have to worry any longer that she will be destroyed. She will never again be tempted by evil or controlled by evil. Satan can't harm anyone who does not possess original sin."

Her revelation left him speechless. Now he understood why the demons only threatened to harm the people he loved and never him personally. They couldn't harm him because he lacked original sin. He was anxious to learn what he must do. "Do I use your church's ceremony? Will you help me?" Josephine was willing to help him with the process. "You are not a priest, so you don't need to use the Catholic ceremony of exorcism. Your special healing powers supersede any such ceremony." Josephine said, "You need to once and for all appreciate God's gift to you; you are going to need the power to heal later in your life."

"Do you know how Balair put Satan into Anne? Do I just pray for her and put my hand on her forehead to undo his violation of her?" She confided, "Undo what he did, as he did. Inhale what he exhaled, exhale what you inhale and then hold her head and pray for her; she will then be free of Satan." He had another question. "Why is Balair going to allow me to do this to her?" Josephine said, "Remember when you were a young man and you would walk by Lake Stamen; the lake would have a soft reflection of moonlight even when the sky was black? Remember when you put your hand in the water on that cold, frigid night, and it was as warm as bathwater?" Ephriam answered that he had remembered all of those things. "Ephriam, Lake Stamen is a refuge. It's been placed there for you. It is a place that is safe from evil; it's a place that Dominique and I have been called to. We warmed these waters 500 years ago. Bring Anne to our cottage. Do what you must do there. Balair cannot harm her there." Ephriam was thankful for the nun's instruction and for her cottage where he could commit the deed. "Ephriam, you possess the Holy Spirit in such a profound way that allows you to heal the sick. I suspect it is because you have been selected an invocator. As clergy, you baptize and save the sinner from Hell. But even more than that, you have the special power to use the Holy Spirit to drive Satan's spirit from those possessed by it, but you must bring it out the same way it entered. You have the power to save your sister. You must do it!"

He visited Dominique. "I don't feel I have the power to drive Satan from anyone." She smiled. "Oh, you have more than enough! And the truth is any person you rid of Satan's spirit will then have profound faith because you will cleanse them of original sin." He felt uneasiness when he heard her say *original sin*. Original sin was what every living person is born with, except a very chosen few. "If it is true I can cleanse someone from original sin, then I will truly accept I have sacred powers." Dominique gave a sigh of relief and slapped her knees with both hands. "Now you finally understand! God blesses us through grace, not because of deeds.

You will pray over Anne, and the Holy Spirit will enter her and wash away her original sin! And she will lose her sinful ways because of God's grace, passed on from you, from your hands!"

As unimaginable as it was, Ephriam realized that the only way he could save Anne was committing this incest; it would take only one minute of terrible sin. Surely God would pardon him for the despicable act of sucking Satan from inside the vibrant and virtuous young woman.

Dominique gave him some instructions. "After you remove Satan from her, carry her to the lake, baptize her and pray over her until nightfall. When she awakens she will be blessed because the Holy Spirit dwells inside her, and her faith will be, from that day forward, forever profound."

At first he thought he could just tell her that she was possessed and what he needed to do to rid her of the evil. If she cooperated perhaps the dreadful act could be committed with very little trauma. However, he doubted she would believe him. Instead, she would see him as vile and despicable; the love and respect she had for him all her life would be replaced by contempt and revulsion. The memories of the wonderful times they shared growing up would be shattered. Also, there was a possibility Anne would attempt to take her own life if she became convinced she was possessed.

He needed to find a way to suck evil from her and replace it with goodness without her ever knowing. It seemed, at the time, impossible.

†

Chapter 19

1848

The exorcism of Anne

He was glad to know Lake Stamen was a safe zone. How did Sister Josephine know about that? How did she know about those cold nights when he tested the warm water under the moonlight? If he was an invocator he might very well need a safe zone. He wondered; did other invocators have safe zones?

He was reading late into the night. Gretchen was concerned when he became more withdrawn than normal. "Dear, can I be of any help? What is troubling you?" He smiled; he always appreciated her concern for him. He only spoke the words that were necessary to put his wife at ease. "I am well, please be patient with me while I deal with problems with which a clergyman must always cope."

He rode out to the lake early the next morning. The sisters were on their morning walk when he caught up with them. "I need to know; are both of you blessed Angels from Heaven?" Dominique was surprised by the question. She turned to Josephine, expecting her to answer. Josephine said, "Reverend, we are here to help you if the need arises." Ephriam needed to hear no more. He silently watered his horse while watching the two sisters stroll around the lake. He always felt at peace when he was at the lake; he had a subtle feeling of contentment.

The next day he went to visit Doctor Taber in Jenkinstown. The doctor was a strange man, short and balding. He seldom smiled and always seemed distant. Despite these quirks, he was well liked by his patients; he was a good doctor.

Wearing his Sunday suit with clergy collar, Ephriam was nervous about the visit. He intended the meeting to be formal between two professionals, setting the tone for his very unusual request.

Sitting in Taber's small cramped office, located in a room next to his parlor, which also served as his waiting room, the two exchanged pleasantries.

"Doctor, I need a small dose of potassium bromide." He had rehearsed making the request. Short, firm, and direct. He sat motionless awaiting the doctor's reaction.

The anticonvulsant properties of potassium bromide had just recently been introduced. Ephriam had read about the compound in a medical journal he requested from the medical college in Philadelphia. The article stated potassium bromide is the first effective medication for epilepsy.

Ephriam didn't care about its ability to treat seizures. He was interested in its side effects, in particular just a few of the side effects - a need to sleep during the daytime, loss of concentration and memory, confusion and headache. The drug was safe, there was normal response to verbal stimulation, and the functions of the heart and lungs were unaffected. The medical journal also stated that the drug was a white crystalline powder, soluble in water. When diluted, potassium bromide tastes sweet.

"Reverend Bernharter, I never expected such a request from any of my patients and certainly not from my pastor." Ephriam kept mum until the doctor finished reacting. "Why would you possibly need potassium bromide?" Ephriam answered, "I can't tell you. It's too complicated to explain, and I'm hoping you will just trust me. I need it; will you give it to me?"

"I'm willing to give you a dose, but I want to remind you I am violating my oath to do so." Ephriam said, "I am aware of that; I would never ask this of you if I wasn't compelled to do so. Someday I hope to explain the circumstances that force me to ask you for this favor."

The doctor did not have any of the drug in his office; he needed to send to Philadelphia for it. A week later he knocked on Ephriam's front door and handed him a white envelope. "Be careful. It is one dose, use all of it. Don't ask me for anymore."

A few days later he invited Anne to ride with him to Lake Stamen. He hitched up the buggy; he planned a picnic. Under a large locust tree along the lake's shore, they would share the food and lemonade and have a chance to talk and reminisce before she left home for adventure in far away places.

Now that he knew the lake was a safe zone, he had renewed self-confidence. It was a warm day, and a summer breeze blew across the water, rushing through the trees, shaking the young limp branches and stirring up the new dark green leaves. The birds were busy building their nests and singing their summer songs while serenading the couple as they sat on the thick blanket, a second one folded and set aside.

He asked, "Are you going to write to me?" She laughed aloud, "Oh dear brother, what a preposterous question. I could not live a day without writing to you!" He believed her. He was always proud to be in her presence. He was always amused watching the men, many times embarrassing themselves, while they vied for her attention, flirting with her, kissing her hand, asking for a dance, not at all hiding their desires to court her, marry her, have her. He knew her better than any other man ever would. He knew her when she was a little girl. He kissed her cuts and scrapes, he helped her wash her face for dinner, he taught her to read, he brushed her long blonde hair. He defended her and made excuses for her when she misbehaved, and he supplied alibis when she was late for Bible study. No other man could ever share moments like those with her. He was the only brother she would ever have. He didn't have to compete with any other man. He was in a category all by himself.

He poured the lemonade, and while she danced barefoot in the thick grass, he put the white powder in her glass. When she fainted, he watched for any onlookers and then wrapped her in the second blanket, hurriedly carrying her into the dense woods.

There under the privacy of the thick trees, he laid her down and opened the blanket. His mind was in a frenzied state. He wondered again what he was doing. Was he insane? Is this how a predator attacks? He had stolen her consciousness; she was completely at his mercy. He could do harm to her. He could kill her!

He sought to suppress all his feelings; the sorrow and guilt he felt for drugging her, invading her privacy, robbing her of her dignity, all because of the evil Balair, that demon, that spreader of hate, that dealer in misery and torment.

He brushed off all these thoughts and concentrated on the job at hand. He had studied the exorcists of the Catholic Church. They teach that demons can be effectively expelled from a possessed person by the formal rite of exorcism. Excorsims can only be performed by bishops and those they designate, or by prayers of deliverance which any Christian can perform themselves. As the evil spirit exits, the person possessed gives off high-pitched screams, and the body convulses and vomits. He would never allow Anne to go through any of these ordeals.

He knew he was doing the right thing. He knew this was the way to rid Anne of Satan, to avoid the Biblical description; *"The evil spirit shook the man violently and came out of him with a shriek."* He leaned over her and looked closely in her ears. He saw the ever so slight blue smoke he had seen before. He put his lips to her right ear and inhaled the smoke. His heart was racing, he was short of breath; the pale blue smoke was burning his lungs. He exhaled, and then started coughing violently; he could see the blue smoke zigzag rapidly through the air, then disappearing. He did the same to her left ear, the coughing was worse now. This was taking up too much time; the drug would soon begin to wear off. He kissed her lips; she opened her mouth slightly, unaware of the intrusion. He took his hand and puckered her lips, put his mouth to hers and deeply inhaled the blue smoke. He again coughed violently. Standing up, he staggered a few feet away and fell to the ground, vomiting. The coughing finally stopped, but he vomited again. Suppressing all the conflicts that had filled his head, he pulled up her dress and pulled down her panties. He now committed the ultimate violation of her. He inhaled once, turned his head and exhaled. The smoke rapidly blew away like a gust of wind: obviously it had some evil destination. He inhaled once again, and once more turned his head and exhaled. Finally it was over. He wrapped her in the blanket and carried her to the lake's edge. Filling his cupped hand several times with water, he baptized her. Then he laid his hand on her forehead and prayed over her for more than an hour. *"Our Father, who art in Heaven, hallowed be thy name. Thy Kingdom come, thy will be done, on earth as it is in Heaven. Give us this day our daily bread, and forgive us our trespasses as we forgive those who trespass against us. And lead us not into temptation, but deliver us from evil, for thine is the kingdom, and the power and the glory for ever and ever, Amen."*

He carried her back to the locust tree and gently set her

down. Suddenly he noticed her skin had an ever so slight glow and that she was smiling while still in a deep sleep. He had the courage to do what Dominique and Josephine told him he must do. He had used an awesome power to give her the Holy Spirit and save her life. For the first time he understood that if he was called to help bring about the Second Coming he was capable to help; he was prepared!

He waited for Anne to regain consciousness. "What happened? I must have fainted!" Making sure not to look alarmed, he gave her a glass of water. She apologized. "I'm very sorry. Can we go home? I don't feel well, I have never had a headache as awful as this." He walked her to the buggy; she was unsteady on her feet, staggering and near collapse. She rested her head on his shoulder during the ride home, the ride she thought was premature. Instead it was the timing Ephriam expected. He couldn't let her know that he also felt sick; he had smelled and tasted Satan. Although he had spit the evil from his mouth, the stagnant, putrid taste from the residue turned his stomach. When they arrived at his house Gretchen wiped her face with a cool wash- cloth and encouraged her to rest until the headache passed. Ephriam went out the back door and walked far into the woods and vomited some more.

The next day Anne awoke early and hungry for one of Gretchen's hearty breakfasts. "I haven't felt this good for a long time, I have the urge to run a race with my brother and perhaps go back to the lake for a swim!" Gretchen was happy she felt so much better. Anne was anxious to be reunited with Robert Krieg. She felt healthy and exhilarated; she was convinced she now had the energy to live the life her lover lived; it was a physically and mentally demanding life, thrilling and dangerous, one filled with sacrifice. It was also a life with real purpose and many rewards. She prepared to give up everything to help him, to be with him.

A few weeks later the family gathered at Ephriam and

Gretchen's house for dinner to celebrate Mary's birthday. Grandparents Henry and Sally and great-grandparents Luther and Rachael were there. Jeanie had been encouraged to take this evening off and attend a choral presentation in Franklinsburg. Ephriam had arranged for her to be the pianist for the program. Only Ephriam knew she could play any musical instrument perfectly.

After dinner, Robert Krieg and Anne came in from the dark outside through the back door. Before anyone could leap to their feet, Anne shouted, "Please, just listen to me for one moment!" The nervous couple tried to make amends before rushing away. "This is Robert, he is to be my husband if Ephriam will marry us right now. We must leave; we're going to Montana Territory to help runaway slaves get to the border and escape into Canada to freedom." Robert spoke in his thick French accent, "I am wanted by the authorities, I have shot two men in self defense, and I have stolen from the corrupt and immoral slaveholders. Let me assure you I am an honorable man who has a mission. I love my dear Anne, and I beg for your blessing." Anne was crying as she turned to Ephriam. He slowly arose and reached for his Bible on the china cabinet. "Let us go into the parlor." He pronounced Robert Krieg and Anne Bernharter husband and wife while the rest of the family stood in stunned silence. Gretchen hugged them both. Ephriam shook Robert's hand and then embraced and kissed his beloved sister. The rest of the family would need time to adjust; changes were coming.

Anne would write every month or so. She told about the many stressful times, the sleepless nights, and the tense moments. She also wrote about the pleasure she experienced seeing the excited looks on the black faces as they contemplated the freedom that was finally only hours away.

Robert would hear the barking dogs, then gunfire as the vicious bounty hunters fired their warning shots that stopped the fleeing blacks in their tracks. They didn't plan to give

Krieg any warning shots; his life wasn't worth anything to the vultures. They would sooner have him dead, doing no more harm.

He and his dozen or so associates came home to Anne and the other women on quite a few of those dark opportune, nights that offered no moonlight bruised from a falling horse, tree branches hitting them in their faces, falling into ditches, down into ravines, or into creeks. There were sprained ankles and broken arms. On one occasion she removed shot gun pellets from his back, and two times she had to summon a doctor to treat serious bullet wounds: one was to his shoulder, the other to his stomach. The stomach wound and resulting loss of blood could have ended his life. Anne always said he refused to die.

She and the other wives also helped nurse the runaways. The escapees would become exhausted from living in tunnels, or in the Krieg's cellar or some other farmhouse, or in a hog pen, or in an underground cave by day, and then running sometimes for hours under cover of darkness during the night. They needed food and water, clean clothing and hot water to bathe. She was particularly sensitive to the suffering the women and children endured during their escape. The women couldn't run as fast carrying a baby or dragging along a young child. The children didn't yet have the long legs needed to run and stay ahead of the predators on horseback.

One night they came looking for Robert. It was very late, after 11 p.m. The three ravagers didn't knock; they kicked in the large oak front door. The children were asleep; Anne had just tended the fire and was enjoying a cup of tea.

She had prepared herself for intrusions by the bounty hunters. She would offer no resistance; she would calmly give false information and answers to their questions, and then hope they would leave. This night, however, they resolved to find him and shoot or hang him. The leader, dirty and unshaven, his clothing filthy and torn, demanded, "Where is that son-of-a-bitch husband of yours?" She shrugged her shoulders. Normally that response would be quite enough; bounty hunters never expected Abolitionist wives to cooperate. This time the leader was a particularly nasty man. He smashed his rifle butt into Anne's head. She turned just as it came toward her face; the side of her head was cracked as she fell to the floor. He was ready to serve another blow, one that would have surely ended her life. The other two stopped him; there was a scuffle; finally they managed to seize his gun.

Just then Robert and two of his men, alerted by the broken door, walked through the doorway with their muskets drawn. Anne got to her feet and assured Robert that she would be fine if he could get the doctor to the house. He sent one of his men for the doctor and then marched the three bounty hunters outside.

Robert Krieg considered himself a warrior, a soldier in a war against a holocaust. He was a radical Abolitionist. He shot dead two of the raiders, and his associate shot the other. He waited with Anne until the doctor arrived a couple of hours later. Her skull had a slight crack; she probably had a concussion. The raiders' bodies were long gone, riding the rapids of a nearby river face down.

How could Krieg, a Christian man who strongly believed in social justice and the dignity of all men, help murder three men? When asked about the violence that was part of his and Anne's life, he would reply, "The fight for the abolition of slavery is a war, in war you must kill the enemy. I kill the enemy."

Years later, after the Civil War ended, moved to Canada and prospered, eventually sending all five of their children to his native Switzerland for their education. Anne sailed with Robert to visit there.

After the end of Reconstruction they once again needed

to be protected from former rebel guerrilla fighters and members of the Ku Klux Klan. Bent on vengeance and financed by robbery and plundering, they plotted to kill people like Robert and Anne who helped the black men, women, and their children sneak through the cold and darkness of night to freedom. They all had a price on their heads.

Later Anne would be honored by many and written about in elementary, high school, and college textbooks. Her name is often mentioned whenever accounts about the heroines of the Underground Railroad are written or told.

Getting Anne married and sent off to Montana gave a happy ending to Ephriam's latest challenge. Now he wasn't distracted while spending the long hours counseling, baptizing, confirming, marrying, and burying his parishioners, and leading them in worship and prayer.

He started to work harder at being a good family man. Gretchen was a wonderful wife; she loved him and understood the sacrifices he was required to make as the church's pastor. Many times the meals she had worked hard to prepare went uneaten by him because of a family crisis; it was always some other family's crisis. Preoccupied with the trouble of others, his mind wandered when she told him about her and Mary's day.

There were benefits to living such a life. As the pastor's wife, everyone in the community respected Gretchen. She expressed her opinion only when she felt it was wise to do so, withholding judgment when it allowed her to avoid conflict and getting into the middle of situations where members could find a reason to dislike her.

She had a good understanding of human nature, people's strengths and their weaknesses. There was always bad behavior taking place; unfortunately that is a fact of life. She always wanted to be savvy. Maybe she was becoming a little too sneaky, maybe succumbing to the temptation of snobbery; she was acutely perceptive, monitoring Ephriam not only as the pastor, but also how his duties related to him being her husband. She felt confident he would never succumb to temptation with other women, and she headed off the advances and flirtations that were served upon him – not really because of any jealousy on her part, but because of the potential embarrassment that could come his way from some woman's gossipy exaggerations about her fantasies.

Occasionally a man would flirt with her. She was a beautiful woman. The way she wore her hair and the dresses and hats she wore were all fashionable enhancements. What really attracted men to her was her all natural beauty.

Everyday life was good. Ephriam, Gretchen, and Mary were a happy family. Mary became a good student, an accomplished vocalist and pianist, and she enjoyed learning to cook, bake, and especially jarring vegetables and preserves. She had her father's thick brown hair and the features of a German fraulein; she had large shoulders, a big bosom, though still slim and shapely.

Bright and talented, she was sometimes headstrong. She had foresight and a sense of what she wanted to do with her life. She wrote regularly to her Aunt Anne and Uncle Robert. In 1860, when she was seventeen years old, she decided to visit them in Montana. Understandably, Ephriam and Gretchen were against it. Ephriam protested, "There is a war brewing up, and your Aunt is involved with dangerous work." Mary was adamant. Gretchen would only allow it if one of the older women from church accompanied her at Ephriam and Gretchen's expense. It would be a long train and carriage ride. Hilda Noll, Ephriam's retired schoolteacher and first love, and now a family friend, volunteered. Jeanie didn't take Ephriam aside and offer objections to the trip. Unaware that Satan no longer dwelled in Anne, she believed she could still threaten Ephriam to take control of Anne and have her kill Mary and Hilda Noll if by chance he caused her trouble.

Mary and Hilda spent a month in Montana, and traveled to Canada with Anne and Robert. Three weeks later they returned home safe and exhausted. It was a wonderful trip. They got to experience the beautiful sights and sounds of the Western wilderness.

For Ephriam, the last fifteen years were productive and satisfying, but there was always the stress of living with constant fear of Jeanie and keeping his anguish from Gretchen. It was a burden that he had grown so very weary of bearing.

He would pray for a seriously ill child, or a chronically ill old woman, or a man suffering from emphysema, or a young wife suffering a miscarriage, and occasionally he would reluctantly lay his hands on a particularly hopeless case, not telling anyone for fear that Jeanie would find out and kill the patient to punish him for disobeying her; he wasn't allowed to heal anyone.

He would discourage any talk that he was a miracle worker, scoffing at every suggestion; he would remind anyone implying he had special powers that such a notion was blasphemous. A few parishioners that he had helped in that way, as a last resort to save their lives, were a particular problem. They would be so grateful for his healing they often refused to remain silent. The stress that resulted from his plight wore him down.

Civil War broke out. The Southern states were in rebellion. Men were volunteering; soon men were being drafted. Ephriam considered joining because chaplains were needed.

He felt that at his age his place was with his congregation and his wife and daughter. He agreed with the popularly held opinion that the war would be over quickly and that it would stay far away.

†

Chapter 20

1863

General Schurz rides into town

By 1863 the rebellion was taking its toll on the very strength of mind of America. It was a continuing tragedy of such great magnitude. Ephriam had been watching the horror progress week by week. Death talk was everywhere: in the churches, in the country stores, at the feed mill, over the fences of every farm in the divided and warring nation. It was truly a waste of life; the lives of thousands of America's young men were snuffed out. Before they gasped for their last breath, they suffered agonizing pain from injury. Limbs just hanging by their skin, ripped from their joints by explosion. These youngsters lay on the battlefields for days after the Armies moved on to contend in more absurd engagements; they laid and suffered until they finally just died. Many who weren't shot got diseases that stayed with them for years after the war, suffering for the rest of their lives; the effects of the maladies shortened their lives.

On a hot June morning in 1863, Ephriam was awakened to the sound of soldiers marching West through Hamlin. Gretchen was running through the house lowering windows and shouting. "Mary, Ephriam, come and help!"

Jeanie came running in from outside to help the family close up the house to prevent the thick clouds of dust being kicked up by the New York Regiments from entering the house like a thick fog and settling on the furniture. Ephriam helped and then went out on the front porch to watch the parade. As the soldiers passed, many of them waved when they saw his cleric collar. Some shouted, "Reverend, say a prayer for me!" Whenever Ephriam would hear the request he would raise his hand, give the sign of the cross, and recite short blessings.

He shouted to an officer, "Where are you boys going?" The officer called back, "We're going to meet Bobby Lee and run his behind all the way back to Virginia!" Two days after marching through Hamlin, these soldiers fought for three bloody days about forty-five miles south in the town of Gettysburg.

Then he saw Sister Josephine being jostled about by the jerking and bouncing of a wagon she was sitting atop, her habit covered with dust. She had joined the troops while the supply wagons watered their horses at the lake. Ephriam panicked. "Sister, come down here, what are you doing up on that wagon?" A broad smile was on her face, and she waved and called out to him. "I must go South to help, I will see you in a few days, Reverend; please pray for me." He didn't want her to go; he shouted back, "It's no place for you there Josephine; get down from there and come to me." Her face lost its smile, and then she turned away.

Judge Daniel Shank, fearful that the invading confederate army was pillaging his Jenkinstown general store, came riding into Hamlin after finding out that the New Yorkers were the boys creating so much dust it could be seen from the courthouse eight miles away. Soon the village was quiet, still and calm as the sun set, and the excited local residents delayed their bedtimes not only because of the terrible heat and humidity, but many had walked to the village square to discuss what surely was going to be a terrible battle when-ever and wherever the Union Army ran into the Rebels. They worried about what would happen to their town if the Rebels broke through and marched north. One man said, "I hear they kill the cattle, the hogs, the chickens." Everyone was listening intently. "Then they rip off the porch railings and tear up the floor boards, start a fire and butcher right there in the front yard, feeding their men all within an hour or so." A woman spoke up, "I hear they kick in your door, they look for jewelry, for money, and they take liberties with women and young girls." Most had been told about the Rebels tracking through homes with their muddy boots, soiling the furniture with their dirty and ragged uniforms, taking blankets to use on the ground to sleep, and stealing shoes because many soldiers, at any given time, were walk-ing barefoot, their shoes worn out long ago.

The people of Hamlin slept lightly that night, and the next day many of them gathered again at the general store hoping to get news from teamsters traveling north. Some of the men rode to the newspaper offices in Jenkinstown or Franklinsburg hoping to get the latest details coming off the telegraph.

Ephriam spent a long day reassuring many, telling them to pray for the soldiers and to pray for peace. That eve-ning he decided to hold an impromptu prayer service at the church. It was well attended. He left the church and slowly walked home, the effects of his weariness and the stifling humidity slowing his pace. During the next few days, dur-ing that hot, humid weekend, rain clouds hovered over-head, occasionally dropping some raindrops, just enough to tease the people with slight relief from the scorching sun and heat. The distant sounds weren't the clashing of storm clouds; the pounding of the guns driving the whizzing shells through the air sent their sounds of thunder and shook the ground for miles. They were the sounds of war, reminding everyone hard fighting was taking place. On Sunday the thunder stopped, and men racing home from the telegraph office shouted that Lee and his army were retreating; the Bluecoats were chasing him. A small crowed gathered at the store and engaged in noisy celebration.

Late that night, Ephriam sat on the front porch settee, finally getting some relief from the hot, stagnant and sticky air. It had begun to rain heavily.

He had fallen asleep but was abruptly awakened. Startled, he could hardly believe any of his senses that were all at work. Major General Carl Schurz, with an entourage of twenty-four muddy and rain soaked mounted officers and enlisted men, came riding into Hamlin a little after 2 a.m. on July 5, 1863, the horses splashing puddles of water and slinging mud onto the town's porches. Ephriam quickly went inside preparing to calm Gretchen and Mary if they should awake. He was surprised to see soldiers in Hamlin; the telegraph messages reported the defeat of the Rebels and the chasing of them back into Maryland.

A Captain, assuming everyone inside was asleep, pounded on the door. Ephriam came back outside. A short man, soaked and sitting atop his horse, greeted Ephriam. He spoke with a thick German accent, not like the Pennsylvania German dialect, this was a high German accent, the language Ephriam used when he preached during German worship services. Through the heavy rain he could see the two stars on each of the man's epaulets.

"Are you Reverend Bernharter?" Ephriam replied promptly, surprised the General knew his name. "I need you to meet with me immediately. Is there shelter nearby where my men can get themselves and our horses out of the rain?"

Ephriam quickly saddled up his horse and led the entourage to the abandoned old barn at Lake Stamen. It was located where the creek flowed past the feed mill and into the lake a mile to the East on the road to Farntown. The soldiers quickly dismounted and opened the doors, unsaddled their mounts, lit lanterns for light, and built a fire to aid the drying of their clothing.

Schurz spoke in his thick accent, "Reverend Bernharter, I am on a very dangerous mission, I should be heading South in pursuit of General Lee, but I've been overcome by this urgent need to come here and see a minister in Hamlin, Pennsylvania to treat this here wounded Captain; his name is William Denton." Ephriam glanced over across the barn and saw in the dim light the wounded man on a stretcher. In order to transport him by horseback he had been wrapped in two blankets; one of them was wrapped tightly around his midsection. "I hope you can help him; he can't die, he must live." Ephriam walked over to the man and noticed that he was unconscious. He put his hand on his forehead; he was burning up with fever. He unwrapped the blood soaked blanket and looked at fragments of uniform sticking to the man's body, saturated with dried old blood, and a slow oozing of new. Peeling away the blue fragment pieces, Ephriam saw his protruding intestines, sweat, dirt and artillery fragments mixed in, small-attached pieces of the flesh falling down along side of his body. Ephriam's stomach began to turn. He wondered how the man survived such wounds. He surely should be dead.

He asked the General, "Why didn't you have a medical attendant take care of him? Why did you bring him here to me?" Schurz didn't look pleased; he wasn't going to be very patient with a country pastor. Ephriam kept up his argument. "This man is going to die, he should not have been brought here!" Schurz screamed, "No, Reverend, he's not going to die, he better not die, my men and I have not ridden forty-five miles North in vain!" Ephriam now suspected that somehow General Schurz knew that he could lay his hands on this poor man who was hit by shell and ripped open. "Is this man the son of someone very important?" Schurz was tired; he was trying to be patient and reply to Ephriam's questions. "Reverend Bernharter, coming North here could cost me my commission; I could be court-martialed, especially if this young Captain dies, but even if he lives I have taken a great risk coming here. I don't want to be imprisoned, but I am compelled to do what I must to ensure that this young man is rehabilitated." Schurz was a devout Catholic, having encamped his entire corps on the grounds of a Catholic convent in Northern Maryland during the march to Gettysburg while he dined and prayed with the Mother Superior. The General continued, "I not only take orders from my superior officers, but I also follow God's orders. I know that the only way Captain Denton is going to survive is to be treated by the laying of the hands."

Ephriam asked, "How did you find out about me?" The General's answer was surprising. "A colored Catholic nun happened by as Denton was lying on the battlefield moaning in agony. She said a prayer, and I told her he was my personal aide, my very best officer, that we had a special bond; he had saved my life on two occasions." Schurz said, "He always seemed to be able to communicate in an extraordinary capacity, saving lives during one skirmish after another. He would advise me about some particular detail that time and again seemed to make a difference in our effectiveness in battle and the lessening of our losses of life. We had a closeness of thinking that I find hard to put into words." Ephriam suspected the nun was Josephine. Schurz said, "I looked into her eyes, wishing I could ask for a miracle despite the thousands of other dying men lying on the battlefield. Her name was Sister Josephine; she's the one who told me to go ride forty-five miles North to Hamlin, Pennsylvania and find her friend Reverend Ephriam Bernharter, and perhaps the minister's hands can heal the tragic wounds of Captain Denton." Apparently Josephine somehow knew Denton was special. Schurz continued, "But you are not a priest, how did you and Sister Josephine know each other?" Ephriam explained that at one time they were both devoted to a great man.

He explained to the General, "She lived here, over across the lake in one of the small cottages. She lived with another nun, Sister Dominique, who still lives in the cottage." General Schurz replied, "I will visit her tomorrow, but now Reverend, I need you to pray for Captain Denton, do what you can for him. Try your best, please." Ephriam asked the General if the nun had asked him to deliver a message. Schurz said she had. "Tell the Reverend a miracle is in order."

While two sergeants held lanterns, Ephriam removed some shrapnel and mud with his fingers and then asked for a canteen. He poured water over the wound and pushed Denton's intestines back into his body, unfolding what little skin there was to cover as much of the wound as possible. He laid one hand on Denton's belly and the other on his abdomen and began praying. He felt the air sucked out of his lungs, and as before, his heart was pumping so rapidly it felt like it was going to explode. He kept these sensations to himself so not to alarm the soldiers. The General ordered that sentries be posted; when that was done the other men went to sleep, much needed by these brave warriors who had fought for three days with little or no sleep, and then rode North in a downpour. Trying to get some sleep while sitting up, General Schurz sat with Ephriam while he prayed until 5 a.m.

While keeping his hands on Denton, Ephriam dozed off. A haunting voice of a Shakespearian actor awoke him. He had heard it before and knew who to expect. He turned around and saw Balair standing there, his back tight up against the barn's wall! The demon didn't wait for Ephriam to find words. He still appeared the same, about fifty years old, beaked nose, black rotten teeth and the strong smell of urine and sweat, his feet about twelve inches off the ground and his large tightly wrapped black cape hiding his faint, glowing red body except for his head and hand. Ephriam could see that the freak's eyes were still pink with blood red pupils and that same pale blue smoke was still coming from his ears, nose and mouth, just as it did from Daytrin's.

"Ephriam, you are being very disobedient. You are testing my patience. Perhaps Anne should come home to do some mischief, maybe murder some children or an elderly woman or two! Just think how famous she will become, she will go down in history as the evil possessed Bernharter woman from Hamlin; she'll vilify the Bernharter name for all time." His hideous smirk gave away his evil appetite. "After she makes her mark for history, I'm going to kill her. Maybe I'll torture her to death, or perhaps burn her alive."

Ephriam was scared. One more time he found himself in a situation where he needed to be on the lookout for the demons while laying his hands on someone and praying for them. He chose not to move his hands from Billy Denton's insides; they seemed frozen firmly in place. He could feel the tingling traveling down his arms all the way to his bloody hands, on to his fingertips that were immersed in the gore, and then into Denton's body.

Sunrise came; General Schurz had climbed up into the loft and lied down on the thick straw stored there. He decided he should sleep for 2 or 3 hours. His orders were to be strictly followed; Ephriam was not to be disturbed under any circumstances; he was to pray for Captain Denton for however long it took to save his life.

Sister Dominique was taking her early morning walk when she noticed sentries posted outside the barn. She hadn't seen the one sitting on the roof; he shouted, "Halt, what is your business?" Shielding her eyes, she looked up and shouted, "I live on the other side of the lake, what are you boys doing here?" She didn't wait for an answer; she walked past the two other posted soldiers and opened the large heavy door and noticed Ephriam sitting on the chopping block with his hands on the bloody, mauled soldier. Ephriam jerked and opened his eyes; the door closing behind her startled him. "Sister, it makes me happy seeing you here. I reckon I am in a real fix." She looked over at Balair. Ephriam noticed that she wasn't at all surprised.

He was hesitant to talk about the demon in his presence. "He just appeared, I have had dealings with him before." Dominique knew that, and she knew that the creature was responsible for the abominable blue smoke. While she stared at the pathetic demon she asked Ephriam, "Do you see how his back is up against the wall?" Ephriam had been curious why Balair had not come closer to do something horrible to Captain Denton. Dominique explained, "He can't move closer to you because you are sitting in the safe zone; the whole lake and some space around its perimeter is in the safe zone. The outer wall of this barn sits right on the line; the despicable demon is standing on the line; he can't move any closer!"

General Schurz came down from the loft and smiled broadly when he saw Dominique. "A pleasant sight beholds me! Sister, I am most happy to see you. During the days before entering Gettysburg my men and I spent some time at the convent in Emmittsburg." Their brief stay at the Maryland convent had given them an opportunity to rest, worship, and contemplate the long and costly war they had engaged in to date, and the battles and the resultant death and destruction that will surely follow.

"It is very gratifying to find another angel of mercy among us here in Pennsylvania." Schurz calling her an angel caused her to turn her head and give Ephriam a sudden glance. Catching the glance prompted a sobering thought; he and the General, and the half-dead Captain Denton, were in fact in the presence of an angel. He looked around in search of Balair, but he was gone.

The General said, "Sister, what brings us here is one of your own. On the battlefield she told us we must bring Captain Denton to Reverend Bernharter so that he can be healed; he must not die. Dominique said; "I am aware that Sister Josephine met with you during the chaos. Captain Denton must be saved; he is an important link. May God bless you General, for having the courage to carry out this vital mission."

Ephriam was surprised that Dominique described Billy Denton as an important link. Frank Herr's note talked about links. To Ephriam links meant chains. Was the saving of Billy Denton preventing the breaking of some chain, a chain of events?

It was soon time for Gretchen to wonder where her husband was, although it wasn't the first time Ephriam was away overnight to be with the sick and dying. Dominique said, "I will go visit Gretchen and tell her that you are helping General Schurz with a very important mission, and that you probably will not be home for a day or so." Dominique gave Gretchen the impression Ephriam was providing spiritual guidance to the General. Ephriam was worried Jeanie would get involved. Dominique explained that demons don't know what takes place in safe zones. "Balair is here only because he thought Captain Denton might be outside the line. He won't remember anything about his visit."

Remarkably, for two days, with all the confusion of following General Lee and his Rebel Army to the Potomac, the Union Army didn't question where General Schurz and his men were, and the people of Farntown, kept mostly indoors by the heavy rain, didn't take notice of them in the barn.

The soldiers took advantage of the rest. They bathed in the lake and washed their clothing, taking care of the graybacks (lice). They had survived three days of horrifying slaughter. Many of the men slept on their horses, occasionally one of them would fall off his stead. No one had expected the level of war that would transpire in the little Pennsylvania town that was home to a seminary. Many of Schurz's men were of German ancestry, from Pennsylvania and Wisconsin. The General had been a German revolutionary, fleeing Germany after springing the revolutionary Gottfried Kinkel from Spandau prison. He went first to Paris, then to London. In 1852 he came to America.

He was an excellent orator, earning handsome fees for anti-slavery speeches. He was typical of most Germans in American at the time, adamantly opposed to slavery.

He campaigned for Abraham Lincoln. After Lincoln's election Schurz served briefly as Ambassador to Spain before returning to serve in the war. Lincoln commissioned him a Major General.

Ephriam prayed and prayed in that old barn while the rain noisily pelted the roof. It had been raining non-stop for three days. Schurz barked an order to one of the men. "You go down the road and tell the Reverend's wife that he's up here ministering to some soldiers, and that we're taking good care of him." Ephriam reacted quickly, "No! My wife is accustomed to me being away from home. The nun has talked to her. I don't want anybody in Hamlin to be told of this healing." At first Schurz thought the local people might be southern sympathizers. "I don't like people who are not willing to help us." It was the first hint of confrontation; Ephriam didn't like the General's insinuation. "My neighbors, especially members of my church, support the Union cause. However, it will be better for me if certain evil beings not know about this soldier." The General was curious why. "It's hard for me to believe that Captain Denton is in danger here, nobody knows him." Ephriam was very tired, and now he was the one running out of patience.

"General, I'm sure you realize that some special force has driven you here to find me. Members of an evil force, one in particular who is very dangerous, are dwelling right here in Hamlin and will retaliate in some horrific way if they know Captain Denton was brought here to me to be healed by God's power. They look for any conditions that threaten their evil plans; they are constantly trying to find links to be broken. My healing is a threat because it demonstrates God's presence."

The explanation would have to do. Ephriam was surprised; despite not being able to explain the details, the pious General seemed to understand. The warrior had no clue that Hamlin had become a battlefield, a type he wasn't familiar with. It was the site of a stalemated engagement of good versus evil. To the unsuspecting or the outsider, things didn't appear unusual, but Ephriam and the angel Dominique knew how dangerous it would be for the soldiers to go into Hamlin; they would answer villager's questions as to why they were there; "the pastor is laying his hands on a near dead soldier." Church members that were discouraged by Ephriam to give up their own prayers for his healing would feel hurt by what they perceived as favoritism. Jeanie would overhear and become enraged; she would kill someone; maybe an entire family; probably Gretchen or Mary, or both. She would have Balair go after Anne, and he would discover he had no more power over her; he would be forced to possess someone else close to Ephriam, again probably Gretchen or Mary.

The General said, "Reverend Bernharter, I'll keep my men here at the barn. We are your guests and will do what you say." Ephriam was relieved.

While he sat on one of the bails of hay he had ordered brought down from the loft, seemingly more relaxed now that he believed that Captain Denton might very well survive, Ephriam took the opportunity to question him about the fighting at Gettysburg. "Reverend, it was a terrible affair. It was worse than anyone could have expected or imagined. General Lee is on his way to Virginia, the price we paid to send him home was indeed very high. If Captain Denton survives he will have horrible memories for the rest of his life, as I will, as all my men will." Ephriam knew the narrative he was hearing was one of history being unfurled. He appreciated the General's candor.

"It will take a long time for me to write down my thoughts about the great battle, many men will write about it for years to come. I remember that during the first day of battle Brigadier General Francis Barlow had moved his division into place not where I wanted it, also against the wishes of Major General Howard. But it was where General Barlow wanted to be. He moved his men Eastward across the rear of our defensive line because he evidently became obsessed with a hill about half a mile from the right flank of Brigadier General Schimmelfennig's position. I estimate the hill was about 400 feet high; it was an excellent location for artillery. Without authority, General Barlow moved his 2,500 or so men toward the hill.

He didn't have much confidence in his men; they were of German descent, German like me, and a Pennsylvania German like you Reverend Bernharter." Schurz had so many memories crammed inside his consciousness only a very small amount could ever be shared with others. "I had remembered about a month earlier, when Barlow took over command, he had confessed he had always had contempt for the 'Dutch.'

His skirmish line, followed by the rest of his division, drove the enemy from the area surrounding the hill just as another Union skirmish line waded across Rock Creek east of the road.

General Barlow took the high ground but also outdistanced General Schimmelfennig's ability to support him.

Cavalry was supposed to protect his right flank, but they failed to follow-up.

I saw right away that General Barlow was on his own, and I ordered units to extend eastward to meet his men. Meanwhile enemy cavalry, infantry, and at least a battalion of artillery were setting up his attack.

I knew it was the beginning of the end. The enemy came; one battery after another and one column of infantry after another, threatening to cut me off from Gettysburg and my position on Cemetery Hill to my rear. The guns were making one continuous and awful roar. The air was alive with screaming, bursting shells and flying fragments. With perspiration streaming down their faces, blackened with powder, our brave men kept the guns cool by plunging the sponge-heads in buckets of water. As fast as a man fell another took his place; guns and caissons were blown up, and horses were mowed down and ripped open. Our situation became very critical."

His recounting the hard fighting mesmerized Ephriam. He now wished he had gone off to fight, the thoughts of living the excitement of battle flashed through his mind like a giant dreamlike panorama made so clear by the General's vivid and detailed narrative. "It was at that time Captain Denton got hit by artillery fire; the shell grazed him and kept going, in doing so it tore him open. He was tossed into the air, soaring over one of the battery's guns; two men dragged him under the overhang of some hedging to provide some more cover. It was later I found the nun praying over him. That's when she told me that he must be saved, that I must bring him here to you. I told her that was an impossibility! She looked into my eyes, I shall never forget that penetrating look; her stare overcame me. I'm sure it was a spiritual experience; I felt a warming throughout my whole body; I never had the experience before. I still can't put it into words. It caused any resistance to her demand I might have mustered to fold up." Ephriam was anxious to know her state of mind and how she looked. "She looked very tired, just like every other living and half-living accomplice in the insane gathering, but her determination to offer prayer to the poor souls laying in agony kept her going. She had a diary where she wrote the last words of many who died in her arms. She had promised each one their messages would be sent to their wives, mothers, and children. After I left her I heard that General Meade, after being told she was on the battlefield, ordered an aide to find her and bring her to the relative safety behind the lines at his headquarters. When the aide finally found her and told her she was to be taken to General Meade, she fled; she was shot down and mortally wounded by a sniper while running from him." Ephriam lowered his head and wept softly when he heard the description of her ending.

The General went on, "Captain Denton suffered horrible pain and loss of blood for the rest of that day, then another day of battle, and still another. When the army marched South to pursue General Lee, these men here with me, took Captain Denton and rode hard and fast North to you."

At about noon of the third day in the barn, Billy Denton regained consciousness. Schurz was ecstatic. "Captain Denton, welcome back!"

Ephriam sent one of the Lieutenants assigned to assist him down to the creek for a bucket of water to heat on the fire. He washed Denton's hair and his face, and the deep exposed wound, and then wrapped his midsection with clean bandages made from sheets Dominique had brought from her house. He gave his instructions to the General. "Take the old wagon in back of the barn, put every man's blanket on it, get him laid on it and get about twenty miles from here and find a doctor to stitch up his wound." Schurz said, "Reverend, how can I ever thank you?" Ephriam replied in typical fashion. "General, saying thank you is more than enough. When I can bring God's healing to someone suffering, that's my reward."

To avoid arousing Jeanie's curiosity, Ephriam made a special request. "Would you please not ride back through Hamlin, but instead go out over the back roads?"

He smiled and waved while watching them ride off. He was pleased with what he did, but stress and the resultant depression was quick in making its ugly return, regaining its horrible grip on him. Once more it was becoming part of his everyday life.

†

Chapter 21

1865

The nation is reunited

The Rebellion finally ended with Robert E. Lee surrendering to General Ulysses Grant. All that remained was for the nation to heal its wounds, re-rebuild its economy. Hopefully the people would quickly forget about the issues that had split the nation in two.

The people of the Hamlin area were anxious to have their soldier boys home, and Ephriam welcomed the opportunity to minister to the reunited families. Communities across America were overjoyed that their young men were no longer being drafted into military service, being torn away from their parents or wives and children, sacrificed for honorable cause but needless battle, risking their lives while destroying other's.

The insanity had passed. Now the young men could instead farm their fields, provide for their families, and live a peaceful existence. They came to church to worship, for fellowship, for Sunday school, for suppers, festivals, and the annual Sunday School Picnic.

Ephriam had matured into the type of pastor who melts into the community, becoming one of the very ingredients of it. He was a member of everyone's family. He was the positive influence. From the pulpit he watched as they rejoiced in song, knelt in prayer, and listened intently to his message about Jesus Christ, their Savior. He was their spiritual leader, and he took his role very seriously.

There was always another newborn baby, another baptism, another wedding, and another confirmation of the youth. There were the solemn rites of life, the serious illness, the deaths, the funerals and graveside burials with the tearful cries. He was witness to it all.

During all the years there was the ever-present threat from Jeanie. Many times the rage had built up inside him to the point where he was convinced if she were mortal he would kill her; he would shoot her, stab her, choke her, burn her alive! He could very easily find justification to destroy her any way he could. But she wasn't mortal. He had finally learned to live with her presence in his life. He now considered it an honor that Satan considered him such a formidable threat that he needed to send his demons to watch over him.

Perhaps she was only a very small contributor to evil on earth, but after reading from Frank Herr's work, he came to realize that Satan had planted demons like her everywhere, constantly watching for any appearance of the Second Coming, offering power as a reward to the demon who stopped the return by destroying the new Christ child. Jeanie was a vicious force, and with all the others like her, Satan had reasons to be encouraged.

He talked to her one morning in the garden. "You are getting old, I see wrinkles in your face and gray hair on your head." She started laughing. "Ephriam, stop believing that I'll grow old and die ending our love affair. I'll never do that." She was demonstrating her arrogance as usual. "If I ever decided to have a mortal's death, you would be forced to give me a large, wonderful funeral attended by all the people who would honor me as your loyal servant, the devoted nanny who raised your child, the loyal housekeeper who welcomed the guests to your home. They would pray and thank God for my salvation. You would need to shed tears when you eulogized me; you would tell them that I am in a better place now, and how all who value righteousness will miss me. You would bury me right here in Hamlin; imagine a Nigger demon in Hamlin's white man's cemetery! Imagine me polluting the blessed soil; I would be a sight to behold. It would be quite a gathering of all your Goddamned charlatans!" Ephriam responded, "To celebrate being rid of you I would preach to all those attending your funeral that the Negro girl deserves to rest alongside her own ancestors. Then I would have you put in a cheap wooden box and sent off to some made up address in the Bayou!" She laughed some more.

"The very next day the young girl that arrives at your house, who is then invited in by your wife, who Mary falls in love with, who is then hired to take my place, will be ever cautious not to be too familiar with everything and everybody." Ephriam was forced to listen to yet another Satanic scenario. "That new young girl who all the men will want to fuck will be me!" That got Ephriam's attention. "Did you forget what I told you years ago; I will never leave you!" She continued her harangue, "If I should die a mortal, and my funeral isn't a most solemn ceremony with your passionate eulogy, then before I appear in town as the new young girl, I will find a sleeping young family and axe them to pieces. The devoted husband will die a miserable death. The wife will be forced to watch her children butchered before she meets her end. Your punishment for not respecting me will always cause suffering of the innocent."

He decided from that point on to only engage in necessary conversations with her. No longer would he pretend to not fear her, or make it appear he liked her. No more small talk. She noticed that as he aged he was becoming more resistant to her presence.

"Ephriam, Mary is getting older now, I don't have as much to do around the house. I'm tempted to kill someone every month or so to relieve my boredom. What do you think of my idea?"

He tried his best to ignore her taunting. "Even you wouldn't kill just for the sake of killing. You need to have a reason to kill someone. You need to kill to sustain your awful evil mission." Jeanie turned serious; she knew he was right. "Ephriam, you're a very smart man, that's why you're an invocator."

Ephriam replied, "The war between good and evil is the basis of man's very existence. God has created everything, and that is good. Your master is evil and will someday be destroyed."

†

Chapter 22

1876

Billy Denton returns to Hamlin

Ten years later in 1876, during a Sunday morning church service, as Ephriam was about to give the invocation and call to worship, Billy Denton, his wife Martha, and three of their seven children Anna Mae, Gina, and Billy Jr., walked into the church and sat in one of the pews at the rear of the sanctuary. It was communion Sunday, and when the time came Billy and Martha walked up front to the altar rail, prayed for forgiveness of their sins, and then received the sacrament; Ephriam placed the bread in their mouths and held the cup while they drank.

After the service the church members, as always, filed past and greeted Ephriam. When Billy's turn came he asked Ephriam if he recognized him. Ephriam couldn't recall who he was. "You saved my life pastor, you prayed for me in a barn outside of town. General Schurz brought me here to you." Ephriam turned pale; he now remembered. Jeanie had not come to church with Gretchen and Mary that Sunday, so he had time to figure out how to handle Billy Denton. If Jeanie found out about the healing, even though it was years ago, she would become enraged. She would consider Billy Denton a threat. He wouldn't survive her wrath.

"I can't farm any more, my war injuries have made that impossible." He explained how he, Martha and the children had moved from his hometown, the farming area of Altoona, 150 miles away to Lockdale, just three miles away, to work as a teamster at the ice works and to be near the pastor that saved his life. "Reverend, I suspect you will be ministering to the Dentons for years to come!"

Ephriam told Gretchen and Mary to go home without him; he would follow along later. Sitting across from them behind his desk, Ephriam gave the unusual couple a good looking over. Billy was a big man; he was over six feet tall and easily weighed 250 pounds. Ephriam had remembered him as a young skinny officer. Ephriam noticed while shaking his hand how large his hands and arms were. He had big shoulders, large feet and a sizable neck. There was still some hair on top of his head; his high forehead was an extension of his large baby-face that seemed to be always wearing a broad grin. Martha wasn't beautiful, but she was an attractive woman in a plain, natural way. Ephriam noticed she was easily ten years older than Billy. She had a slender build, a pretty face, golden blonde hair, and hazel eyes. She was outspoken. Ephriam quickly realized that Martha was always willing to give her opinion and exercise her influence over her husband. For a wife and mother her age she was remarkably thin. Ephriam observed her small breasts that didn't appear to sag; one wouldn't expect a woman who nursed seven children to have breasts protruding like hers. Like many women of her day, Martha could be dainty and so very feminine, but she also helped work in the fields, fed the animals, did the milking, helped with the butchering; she helped her husband when and where needed. Martha's ability to do hard physical labor was of particular importance because Billy's war injuries limited his ability to do farm work, lift things, to lead a team of horses, even to pitch hay. Ephriam concluded that Billy Denton was lucky to have found Martha Darby.

Ephriam obviously never thought he would see Captain Billy Denton again. Faced with the fear that he had lived with for years, he wondered what would happen if Jeanie found out he had healed Billy right under her nose in the safe zone. "Billy, I discourage people from relying on these special powers I have. They need to put their faith in God and the Bible, not me. The church frowns on pastors claiming such powers; I could be excommunicated." They listened to him intently. "You must never tell anyone about those days that I prayed for you; there is a lot more at stake than you realize. Do you understand?" Billy and Martha assured him that they understood.

They set up housekeeping in a small house just East of Lockdale along the road to Franklinsburg. As was Ephriam and Gretchen's custom, after new families moved into the area and got settled, they were invited to the Bernharter house for supper. The Denton clan was anxious for this special event.

Martha had four children from her previous marriage to a William Darby, who followed the Mormon faith. After she married him she gave birth annually until Darby decided in 1864 to pack up the whole family and move to Utah and take another wife or two.

Martha refused to go. She threw him out and somehow for the next two years paid rent and fed and clothed her children. She took in laundry, cleaned houses, and did sewing.

When Billy came home from the Army after spending almost a year in an army nursing home she took him on as a boarder. He began doing odd jobs in the area but could barely afford to pay her.

The doctors had told Billy that he would never be able to satisfy a woman sexually or have children. Martha was comfortable with those circumstances; she was twenty-four years old with more than enough children.

She and Billy would have long talks about the joys and hardships of life, her about her marriage to a Mormon, and him about his experiences in the war. "You kept thinking everyday that this could be your last day on earth. Bullets would wiz by your head. I rode horseback because I was an officer. I would have rather walked with the enlisted men; you got to keep lower, a lesser chance of getting picked off. You'd watch your men get shot, get sick, suffer from dysentery, all the time the enemy, those Goddamned Johnny Rebs would keep coming after us. We'd sneak up on them and kill as many as we could just to get even for what they did to us the day before. Once in a while we'd get to face each other on an open battlefield, or one with trees that we could use for cover. During those battles there were many casualties; we'd just shoot each other to death for no Goddamned reason. Those poor Johnny Rebs were fighting to protect the rich land owners, the slaveholding sons-of-bitches, while their wives and children back home didn't have enough to eat." He'd keep talking until he got all the resentment out of him. That relief would only last a little while, maybe a day or two, until it welled back up inside him again. Martha was a good listener, she never interrupted him; the war was the one subject she never gave her opinion about, not to Billy, and out of respect for him, not to anyone else. She let him talk about the war to anybody who would listen; she knew it was good therapy. What he said about it was what she came to believe as the truth. As he aged, like the thousands of other veterans, Billy's accounts of the war became fuzzier.

She would tell him about her marriage to William Darby. "William was raised in the Mormon faith. When I was being raised I was taught that beliefs accepted after the New Testament are the beliefs of cults, Mormons included."

Billy didn't know anything about that. "I just know that it is not fair to a woman for her man to have other wives, it just is not right."

She'd reflect, "In many ways he was a good man; he was a good provider; he worked hard. He was a good father; he disciplined the children, but he also praised them when they did well. But he loved sex a little too much. I probably would have been pregnant all the time if I would have stayed with him. If I wasn't willing he just took. He said that he had the right because he was my husband. I think the reason his family is Mormons is so the men can have more than one woman. I think that's the only reason William stayed with the church." She continued, "One day I got up and just felt different about him. I didn't love him any more. I didn't want him around any longer. It's hard to describe. I took my vows, and I would have stayed with him no matter what, except when he said we're moving to Utah and there would be more wives. I didn't react like I thought I would. I didn't threaten him or become enraged; I thought maybe I would hit him over the head with a shovel! But instead I was relieved. I didn't cry at all the day he left."

Billy said, "My only sorrow is that I'll never be a father. That's my one regret that I'll always live with." Martha asked, "Just what did the doctors tell you?" Typically, Billy was reluctant to talk to anyone about this subject, especially to a woman. But Martha was different. He could talk to her about anything. "They just said that my man parts don't work because of being shot up. They said I'm lucky to have my dick."

Months later Billy asked Martha, "Do you think sometime we could hold each other?" Martha replied with a sigh, "Oh Billy, I don't know whether that would be such a good thing."

A few nights later he was sitting at the kitchen table smoking his pipe and reading about the Indian wars. Martha walked into the room and said, "Why don't you come to bed?" Billy replied, "I'm going to read a little more." Martha said, "I mean why don't you come to *my* bed?"

Martha proved the doctors wrong. Ten months later Anna Mae Denton was born.

He told Ephriam, "I know most men are proud of their children, but I think the thrill was more profound for me because I never expected to ever be a father." Ephriam was impressed with Billy's sincerity and depth of character. "Being in battle prompted me to offer prayers of thanks to my maker everyday since I was wounded, and to ask God to bless you, the minister who saved my life." All wars are horrendous, but Ephriam knew the American Civil War would be one that caused more loss of life, more lost limbs, and the spreading of agony to thousands of families on the streets and alleys of the cities and on the farms in every valley. Billy said, "I longed for the day I could come and see you, to thank you."

As soon as Anna Mae was born Billy and Martha got married. They had two more children - Billy Jr. was born in 1868, and Gina in 1870. Billy would always joke about how easy it was for Martha to get pregnant. "If I look at her a certain way, she'll be with child!" Martha took the kidding in stride; she knew it was her husband's way of bragging. "It takes a lot more than a look to get me pregnant Billy Denton!"

Ephriam was now happy to have the Dentons in his fold. They led active lives. Billy was always busy; Bobby and Kenny went to school and helped with the outside chores. Martha had her hands full cooking, baking, doing laundry and mending; daughters Carol and Marie helped with the younger children. At church the family helped fill out the adult and children's choirs and always attended Sunday school. The older children helped with church suppers and went along on home visitations; the younger ones were altar attendants. Martha served on quite a few committees; Billy served as a lay minister and sat on church council.

† Chapter 23

1885

Ephriam retires

In 1885 Ephriam decided to retire. He had wanted to write for years and thoroughly study Frank Herr's research papers. He planned to preach to different congregations as a Senior Pastor. He was excited about that. He and Gretchen had always enjoyed visiting other churches and having fellowship with new groups.

He could also adopt church projects that particularly interested him. He would assist in fund-raising for a new church building, a new Sunday school, raise money for an orphanage or almshouse. He would have plenty of worthwhile work to do without enduring the day-to-day grind of ministering to one congregation.

They also planned a trip to the Canadian mountains to see Anne and Robert. The Kriegs by now had become involved in the newspaper publishing business. Robert and Anne founded a small newspaper in the isolated Canadian valley they lived in, eventually moving to larger towns as they bought larger newspapers. Anne eventually had five children and founded an international human rights organization. She traveled to Europe and Africa numerous times to head up causes aimed at combating genocide and other humanitarian causes.

One day Ephriam was returning from a home visit when he noticed Jeanie standing in the middle of the road. He was surprised to find her over two miles from the house. After he pulled up the horse and stopped the buggy, she walked over to him and stated, "I am leaving, you can say goodbye to Gretchen and Mary." Ephriam said, "When you say you are leaving, what exactly does that mean? Are you leaving my life?"

"Ephriam, you'll never learn! I told you before I will never leave your life, but it's time that I do some work other places. I'm not so sure you have been a selected invocator; you have become nothing more than an old worn out peddler of bullshit."

Ephriam had kept the existence of Frank Herr's note from Jeanie for forty years. He had come to believe that he might be *the* invocator, the very one who will assist God with the Second Coming.

He wanted to jump out of the carriage, fall to his knees and shout to Heaven his thanks. He felt like thousands of pounds had been lifted from his shoulders. He believed that without Jeanie around he could have peace. He restrained himself, showing no outwardly signs of jubilation. He didn't want to make her angry; she could change her mind very easily.

She showed her wicked smile. "Let's fuck just for old time's sake, what do you say?" Ephriam froze, struggling to keep his face blank of emotion. "Ah, forget it. You're lousy at fucking. You're a lousy minister, a lousy husband, a lousy father, you're a waste of my time!" He couldn't resist responding, "Yes, and you're a murderer!" The wrath he expected from her never came. Instead she seemed to be in a melancholy and reflective mood. "I know you fooled me a few times over the years. You got away with that." He said, "All these years I only tried to help people, I've tried to comfort their souls and their bodies despite having to put up with you."She gave her warning, like she always did when she was losing an argument. "Don't ever give me a reason to come back here. I'll cause an earthquake to swallow up this whole Goddamned town with everyone in it; you know I can do it."

She walked to the back of the carriage. Ephriam waited for her to come around on the other side. She didn't. She was gone.

Gretchen was disappointed when she heard Jeanie was gone, especially without saying goodbye.

Mary was heartbroken. Jeanie had been a part of her life from the time she was born. To Ephriam, Mary's love for Jeanie was the ultimate mockery to his fatherhood.

Mary had graduated from the University of Pennsylvania in 1865. She had earned a degree in anthropology, choosing a career that by this time had her traveling the world doing research and writing books. She would come home and stay for a month at a time, and many times go off to Canada to spend time with her Aunt Anne and Uncle Robert.

✝

Chapter 24

1905

The death of Ephriam

In the fall of 1905 Ephriam had gotten very sick. His heart was failing. Dr. Raybold told Gretchen and Mary there was nothing that could be done except make him as comfortable as possible. Mary postponed a trip to South America to help her mother care for him. Anne wrote Gretchen to tell her she was planning a trip home for Thanksgiving.

On October 27th Ephriam died in his sleep.

Newspapers, local and distant, carried his obituary; his funeral was attended by hundreds of people. The church could not hold them all; the large stained glass windows were opened to allow those standing outside to hear the eulogies. The procession to the cemetery was a long one. Ephriam was laid to rest next to his parents and grandparents.

Gretchen had telegraphed Anne with the sad news. She hurried home, intent on spending at least a month with Gretchen and Mary.

Gretchen took his death hard; her life had revolved around Ephriam's ministry. Having many friends, and her family in Philadelphia, helped, but no longer being a minister's wife would leave a great void. She was thankful for

Mary and Anne to help her through the mourning. She had a request for the two women. "I would appreciate if you would go through his papers, sort them and catalog them. It will take some time. Would you do that for me?"

When they walked into his office they realized that it would be no easy task. Anne said, "I'll write to Robert and the children and tell them I will be spending the holidays here." Gretchen's reaction was typical. "No Anne! I can't ask you to be away from your family at Christmas!" Mary expected her mother's reaction. Over the years her father had helped thousands of people, but it was still difficult for Gretchen to accept help from others. Anne replied, "I won't be away from my family for Christmas, I grew up right her in this house, you and Mary *are* members of my family." Gretchen seemed to be giving in; she knew she needed Anne's help. Anne said, "Listen Gretchen, I'm an old woman. I've always tried to do things that made a difference, now I need to do this for my brother, and for you and Mary. Let me help."

It was decided that Anne and Mary would begin the process of organizing Ephriam's books and papers. He had done a lot of writing over the years. The historical societies and the Lutheran Church archivists wanted some of the material. Gretchen would depend on Mary and Anne to choose who received bequests. Much of it would be given to Mary; Anne would get some, and Gretchen would retain the mementos and family heirlooms.

It also was decided Anne would be the chief. She had worked for years in the newspaper business; she had honed editing and cataloguing skills necessary to undertake the project. His papers had been in disarray for many years. Books were stacked on the floor, on the chairs, on the windowsills. Papers were piled high on his desk covering the entire surface; working space was scarce. It was a challenge just to walk into the room without overturning a stack of books or walking on loose, important looking documents lying on the floor. He didn't take the time to file away papers, and many times had to search for days to find an important note he needed.

To Anne's amazement, she discovered a thick diary on the top shelf of the tallest bookshelf. It was a diary that Ephriam had made entries in for years, not everyday, but often. Putting it on the high shelf kept it out of the hands of a visitor's browsing; she suspected he wanted it read only after he died. She asked Gretchen, "Did you know Ephriam kept a diary?" Gretchen didn't seem surprised. "I never intruded in Ephriam's work. I stayed out of his office here at home and certainly at the church. I knew he needed his professional privacy."

After a few days Anne and Mary had made a dozen or so piles of material, sorted into vague, tentative categories. One pile consisted of Frank Herr's thickly stuffed leather bag containing at least a thousand pages of typewritten notes. Anne considered the notes a frantic account of those old scrolls the institute allowed him to research. After reading only one or two pages she got the feeling the man was writing against the clock, trying to record his findings as quickly as possible before his demise. Perhaps he knew his death wouldn't be one portrayed by a candle burning out slowly, the flame flickering away, bringing darkness to the room. He also didn't want his death to come suddenly. He wanted a few days to write his closing; he didn't want to die with an unfinished sentence on the last page.

"Gretchen, did Ephriam read Reverend Herr's research papers?" She replied, "He always wanted to read them; he told me he wouldn't read them until he had nothing else to concern himself with; they would overwhelm him, and he needed to be prepared for the revelations they surely contained." Anne asked, "Do you know if there is an index?" Gretchen said, "Oh yes, but Ephriam said the index wouldn't help anyone understand Herr. His writings must be read from beginning to end, not in bits and pieces."

The writings pulled Anne into his world. At first she was sure she didn't understand anything he was saying. She read and reread, slowly beginning to trust her interpretations. Ephriam was right; there were revelations. However, Anne intended to use the index. She wasn't interested in Frank Herr's revelations that didn't have some impact on Ephriam's memory, Gretchen, Mary, and perhaps herself, and the village of Hamlin.

He had not written predictions based on faith and Biblical prophecy. He wrote everything as sure fact. He knew what was coming - the Second Coming of Jesus Christ. He knew Judgment Day was close, within a hundred years. Anne was fascinated by his certainty. She was determined to piece together the puzzles.

She was shocked to learn that Frank Herr told Ephriam he was destined to have a role in the Second Coming. Anne learned that Ephriam never doubted Frank Herr's assertion that he was an invocator; he was convinced Herr knew what he was talking about.

Anne realized the more she studied Frank Herr's theories and conclusions the easier it would be for her to understand them. She also wanted to know what prompted Ephriam to gain total trust in the old man. She suspected he wrote about that in his diary, and she began reading it between bouts with Herr's passages. She was confident Ephriam's own words would eventually shed light on the intensity of his loyalty to the professor. While leafing through the diary, Anne was shocked to read the entries about her being possessed, how he had discovered her that night in Harrisburg, and years later exorcizing Satan from her. She never realized she was possessed, and she never knew what her brother was forced to do to free her from Satan's grip.

Anne threw the diary across the room. Mary, wondering what she discovered, picked it up from the floor and began reading it in search of other shocking revelations. She found some interesting entries her father had written about saving a soldier who was badly wounded and was brought to Hamlin in the middle of the night.

"He was wounded so badly he should have been dead on the battlefield. They brought him to me because Sister Josephine sent them to me. It was then that I fully understood the two nuns were placed in my life; they made the water warm at Lake Stamen 500 years ago, making it a safe zone that allowed me to heal the Captain."

Mary asked, "I wonder who this soldier was?" Anne suspected that Mary shouldn't be reading everything her father wrote. "I think it's best not to pursue that question." Mary prepared to read aloud. Anne interrupted, "Mary, we have a lot of work to do, read that later." Anne took the diary and placed it in her bag; she decided she would read the most intimate and private revelations in her room at bedtime. Keeping the book to herself, under her control, would enable her to decide what people would know and what they would not know about Ephriam's life.

Anne was reading from early morning right after breakfast, not stopping for lunch, until after supper. In bed she continued to read the diary.

By now she concluded that Ephriam was living a life of great stress. Evidently demons had come to Hamlin to insure that his participation in the Second Coming be muted.

She learned that the soldier was Captain Billy Denton! Gretchen and Mary had known him and his family for many years. They were devoted members of the congregation. Ephriam wrote, *"I had to make sure Jeanie didn't know what I was doing. Balair made an appearance, but was powerless because of the safe zone. It was then that Dominique reminded me about she and Josephine being angels and how the demons are worried about being banished into non-existence if they fail to accomplish their mission. That mission was to prevent me from involvement in the Second Coming of the Lord."*

Anne was stunned. Jeanie Belvoir was a demon! She was thankful that Mary had not read more of the diary. Jeanie had raised Mary; she was the most influential person in her life. She nurtured her, bathed her, dressed her and read to her. She took her to school, taught her about flowers, about trees and the birds, about so many things. She walked her to church. She was the center of Mary's world. Mary loved Jeanie Belvoir. The truth is Jeanie Belvoir was a demon whose sole reason caring for Mary was to hold her hostage. Mary was allowed to live because Ephriam allowed Jeanie to control him!

Anne decided to protect Mary; she would be devastated if she knew the truth about Jeanie. She tore the pages about Jeanie out of the dairy and tossed them into the fire.

The more she read Frank Herr's massive notes, the more eerie she started to feel. She had always believed demons could be cast away. She was confident her faith would sustain her against them. What she feared was the unknown; how large of a standoff was to be revealed, ready to explode into full crisis? Could the end of the world, the Day of Judgment, happen in this little village of Hamlin? She wondered to what extent the demons were invisible. If she didn't know where they were or what they were doing, she couldn't confront them. Jeanie had left Hamlin long ago; or had she? Anne suspected she was present in invisible form.

If anybody was up to the challenge of confronting the demons it was Anne Bernharter Krieg. She was a gutsy woman who had faced danger and confrontation many times in her past. She wrote a long letter to Robert. *"My Dear Husband; I am faced with some problems here. I think my brother dealt with some very serious challenges that he kept secret for many years. The circumstances are very complicated, and probably if explained in detail to you, unbelievable. But I feel there are very real spirits at work here, and unfortunately many of them are evil. I shall carry on until I have sorted everything out for Gretchen and Mary."*

Robert wrote back. *"Knowing you as I do, I am convinced you will journey wherever your suspicions and beliefs take you. Please be brave, please be cautious. I will see you soon."*

Anne took Robert's words as encouragement and consent for her to proceed. She decided she must somehow fully understand what went on in Ephriam's life and try to bring closure to it all.

†

Chapter 25

1905

Anne confronts Daytrin

Anne loved to take long walks. It was on one of her strolls along the creek that flowed from Lake Stamen that it occurred to her what part Ephriam played in all of this intrigue. He was used to save Billy Denton Sr. because a Denton descendent was going to play a very important part in the Second Coming.

Occasionally after supper she would walk to the church and play the organ for an hour or so.

One warm evening while she walked home, the event she had been waiting for took place; the first of the demon creatures made its appearance. Hanging upside down from a limb of one of the big oak trees that lined the main street was this vile creature; she came to learn his name was Daytrin. He was about five feet tall; she could smell him fifty feet away. He began to growl while leaping from branch to branch, shaking the entire tree, and then somehow wrapping his long bony feet around a small branch and hanging like a bat over her head. His head began to glow, then it became dark again; he appeared to be dwarf like with red bristled hair, ashen scaly skin and pink eyes with blood red pupils; a blue smoke was emanating from his ears, his nose, and the corners of his mouth. She watched the upside down creature fondling his penis while he sprayed foul smelling dark yellow urine onto the street; he had vomit dripping to the ground from his mouth.

She looked up and down the street, hoping nobody else would see or smell what she was being forced to endure; Hamlin was temporarily under siege. She felt sick, but she remained calm and walked past him. Surprised by her reaction, he called out "Old lady, you should show some respect; I own you." She kept walking; she suspected ignoring him would infuriate him. Finally she fainted from the effects of the stench; she fell to the ground.

She came to only seconds later, lying flat on her back. He began to growl again. "Satan owns you Annie, dear old, wrinkled and dried up Annie. I warned your brother when I visited him when he was young not to interfere with our work." Anne responded, "Work? What work? You do no work; all you do is try to scare people. You don't scare me, and my name is not Annie!" Anne was indeed scared, but after many years of fighting social injustice using radical, often violent methods, she had learned from an expert, Robert Krieg, to hide her fear, deceive the adversary into thinking she had an overwhelming amount of self-confidence, and then defeat the enemy with a devastating offensive. Robert Krieg often stated his strategy as "I never say fight or flee, I say fight and then flee!"

She asked the demon, "Why are you here? What do you want?" Daytrin's poisonous presence was so toxic she could see that the leaves were withering and dying on the tree.

Daytrin groaned; "I'll not let the evil spirit escape from you; you will not shake violently, the evil spirit will not come out." Still on her back lying in the street, and barely conscious, she began to pray; *"Our Father who art in Heaven, hallowed by thy name."* Daytrin roared. "Stop!" She kept praying. *"Thine kingdom come, thy will be done."* He yelled at her. "Stop! I order you to stop!" She screamed, "You fool, Ephriam sucked Satan from me years ago, and you didn't even know it; you're a fraud, a miserable failure! Satan will never forgive you!" She screamed louder. "I'm calling on him to judge you right here and now!"

He was starting to moan. "You are a liar!" Anne kept up her prayer. *"On Earth as it is in Heaven. Give us this day our daily bread and forgive us our trespasses as we forgive those who trespass against us."* She was getting louder now. "Daytrin, you are my trespasser, you are a failure, and now Satan knows it. I was freed of his horrible spirit; you cannot harm me because of my faith in Jesus Christ, my Savior! I am possessed not by evil but by the Holy Spirit; I am without original sin!" He was panicking now. "Please, don't lie to me anymore!" Anne, still lying in the street, finished her prayer. *"And lead us not into temptation, but deliver us from evil."* She kept her eyes on his. "I've been delivered from evil Daytrin, I am thankful to my Lord and to my brother for that." She was surprised that he had become quiet and calm. *"For thine is the kingdom, and the power, and the glory, forever and ever, Amen."*

He said no more. His eyes were getting darker. She sat up and slid back, away from the tree. She was covered with dirt; her dress was soiled and torn. Suddenly the creature began to glow again, much brighter than before. The glow was not red like his eyes had been; this was a blinding white light and it lit the entire main street of Hamlin. Anne shielded her eyes while trying to see what was happening up in the tree. The heat became intense, and soon the tree was on fire. Suddenly the light disappeared, and a blackened piece of foul smelling matter fell to the street. When it hit the ground she noticed it had become nothing of substance, just a pile of ashes. People, who had come out of their houses frightened by the bright light, now brought buckets of water to throw on the tree. The men helped pump water from the town well to fight the fire.

Anne watched as people raced past the pile of black ashes. She watched it disintegrate, the night breeze blowing little by little of it down the street then swirling into the air until it scattered here and there on the pastures. The black dust killed the grass wherever it settled until the sun bleached the evil from it, turning it white. Satan had punished the creature Daytrin. There was no place for him to go. His existence ended.

The town's people questioned Anne; they wanted to know what started the fire. Anne lied; she told them she saw the tree already on fire when she started to walk by. She said the bright light must have been caused by parts of the tree exploding.

Mary raced down the street looking for her. She was accustomed to seeing an elegant, neatly dressed aunt. What she saw now was a tired and dirty old woman who needed a bath and a bed. Anne told her, "I got dirtier than this many times in my younger days; I fought some hard battles in my life."

She was exhausted, but just before dawn she was up and about; back in Ephriam's office reading, sorting, and cataloguing.

†

Chapter 26

1905

Anne visits Dominique

She decided to visit Dominique. Dominique had continued to teach school and live in the cottage at the lake. Anne needed some help from the nun if she was going to solve the mysteries that had been lingering over Hamlin like a large, gray cloud. "I am convinced Hamlin is under siege and could possibly be terrorized." She was surprised Dominique agreed with her.

The nun didn't let old church doctrine confuse the issues here. "There is no doubt that God selected Ephriam for some important work. Before the Second Coming can take place, everything for hundreds and hundreds of years, which is just a few seconds to God, must fall into place. A missing link, such as a family line that ends prematurely can prevent the immaculate conception." Anne's face brightened. "And Ephriam's mission as an invocator was to save Billy Denton's life because a descendent of his will give birth to the Infant!" Dominique smiled and nodded. "It appears that is so. That is why General Schurz and his men brought Billy Denton from Gettysburg to Hamlin that rainy night. Sister Josephine knew that Billy Denton had to survive his wounds.

She and I were destined to come here because of the safe zone. I watched events unfold leading up to Reverend Herr coming to live and write in the safe zone after he had proven his theories. By publishing them and counseling Ephriam he would have gotten Hamlin through its crisis. It would have been a wonderful time of celebrating God's love. I am now convinced Reverend Herr would have come here if Satan had not had him murdered."

"Why wasn't he told about all this?" Dominique said, "When one lamb wanders away it will stay lost without the shepherd's help. The shepherd uses his staff to lead the lost lamb back to the fold. Reverend Herr was a shepherd. His staff was his faith. While reading the ancient scrolls he struggled with pre-determination; he concluded that events control man, man doesn't control events." Anne was listening and trying to concentrate, but her mind was wandering wildly. Dominique continued, "Many things must remain unknown. The staff will show us the way; faith in God will lead us to our destination and conclusion. Always remember that God is a mysterious God."

To Anne that was a lot of church double-talk, but she kept silent. Her usual response would be confrontational, but she didn't want to show any disrespect or lose Dominique's cooperation. She needed her knowledge and insight.

Anne had more questions. "Ephriam wrote in his diary that Balair came to the barn while Billy was being healed. Why didn't he cause Billy Denton trouble later?" Dominique answered, "Balair didn't want Satan to know about Billy Denton's healing because Satan had charged him with stopping Ephriam from using his power on anyone. Failing to control Ephriam could have easily led to Balair being destroyed. Remember, we are not sure if a Denton family member, perhaps one hundred, or two hundred years, or maybe a month from now, will give the birth. There are many invocators protecting family lines." She gave Anne some more background information. "I knew every word Reverend Herr ever wrote about the ancient scrolls. Even though Sister Josephine was his research assistant, I was much more than his personal assistant. He read to me for hours; and when his eyes grew tired, I read to him. He asked for my opinions. I came to believe every theory, every logical conclusion, every word he ever spoke or had written. Josephine did his research; I helped him keep it coherent in his mind."

Anne appreciated being told more about Frank Herr. Then Dominique told her things that were very scary.

"The unimaginable horror of men killing each other in such numbers, in such grisly fashion, during that battle at Gettysburg was arranged by Satan to eliminate hundreds of suspected links. I'm sure Balair could tell us the exact number of men butchered on the battlefield that were suspected of being an ancestor to the young woman who will give the birth. Thousands of children were never born because of the slaughter at Gettysburg. Because Billy Denton was being watched by an angel, and was saved from certain death, there is a very good chance the young woman who will give the miracle birth will be from him."

Anne said, "And when it happens, the path to the judgment day will begin to be upon us? Satan will be destroyed?" Dominique nodded in agreement.

Anne had some questions about Jeanie. "Where did she go?" Dominique's response was surprising. "She didn't go anywhere. She spent too many years living in Hamlin, caring for Mary, being a member of the Bernharter's household staff. Demons don't age. They can make themselves look older cosmetically, as Jeanie did, but eventually people would have wondered why she wasn't getting any older. To resolve that dilemma she became transparent." Anne never gave this possible complication a thought. "So Jeanie doesn't have a choice; she must stay transparent." Dominique nodded. "Anne, until the second miracle occurs, Jeanie will not stop searching for the virgin. Unless she is stopped she will kill the girl. Once the conception takes place it will be too late; the young girl will be touched by God and become an angel; it will be too late for Jeanie to kill her. There are answers to all these mysteries. Your strong faith is beginning to reward you with insight; my telling you all these things is giving you that insight. Now it will all make sense." Then Dominique made another startling pronouncement. "You are a player in all this Anne. Ephriam saved you not only because he loved you; you needed to be taken back from Satan so you could play your role in all this. Satan had you possessed because you were predestined to play the part you now find yourself playing." Anne reacted to her heart pounding by patting herself on the chest. "You mean God has selected me for something." Dominique said, "Your brother put the Holy Spirit inside you, you are indeed special."

She wanted to know who killed Frank Herr. Dominique didn't hesitate. "Jeanie killed him, and she killed the poor, innocent and devoted couple who tended his house. She not only killed Reverend Herr, she mutilated him. She cut out his tender heart, sampled his flesh and drank his blood, spewing it all over the walls; she is a vicious killer. I'm sure she has killed many." Anne felt queasy. She was tired and wanted to go home.

"I figure Balair is in trouble because he failed to tell Jeanie about Billy Denton's healing in the barn. If she had known, surely she would have killed Denton, and probably General Schurz, maybe even all the men." Dominique said, "The horses too!"

Anne had not been getting much sleep since starting the project. The evening after her visit with the nun was especially restless. She wondered how she could warn the young girl who in the future is going to give the world the second infant Christ.

She resumed her reading at sun-up. Gretchen brought

her some tea. "Anne, I think you need to take a few days away from this and get some rest." Anne, sitting in Ephriam's rocking chair with papers on her lap, gazed out over her spectacles and looked up at the concerned Gretchen. "Maybe yesterday morning I might have listened to you. Talking to the nun has put renewed urgency in getting this morass of ideas and speculation, faith, mystery, and destiny put into some kind of order, not only in file cabinets, but in my mind as well." Gretchen was silent; her only response was a worrisome look on her face. Anne said, "Gretchen, I'm fighting here for my sanity."

Anne found Dominique's observations about Gettysburg intriguing. She reached for a thick book on the shelf titled *"The Ultimate Battle for the Union."* Checking the index, she turned to a page that mentioned General Schurz and was attracted to the portrait of General John Reynolds on page 381. Reynolds was a Pennsylvanian, born only thirty-five miles away from Hamlin. A Confederate sniper shot him on the first day of the Gettysburg battle. Anne took note how handsome he appeared in his 1841 West Point graduation portrait. He looked the part of the cavalier warrior, the epitome of chivalry. She suspected he was a link. Since he had no children, his killing broke the Reynolds chain; that family's line could never be extended to the young virgin girl.

She wondered which soldier with the Fourteenth Tennessee Regiment could claim General Reynolds as his victim. Anne read that bullets were flying furiously. It would not be possible for any one of those Tennessee sharpshooters to know if they fired the fatal shot.

The Reynolds story became more interesting when she read that a woman named Catherine Hewitt, when hearing that General Reynolds had been killed, traveled to Philadelphia and revealed to the family that they had been secretly engaged to be married. When his body had been prepared for the funeral, the family had discovered a locket around his neck and a ring on his finger with the inscription "Dear Kate." Ms. Hewitt's arrival explained to the family the circumstances surrounding the locket and ring. They embraced her, and welcomed her as part of the family. She had told the story of how her and John had agreed that if something happened to him she would enter a convent. Heartbroken, Catherine Hewitt went to Emmitsburg, Maryland to enter a convent called the Sisters of Charity. It was the same convent devout Catholic General Carl Schurz and his Third Division had spent time while marching to Gettysburg! Kate kept in touch with the Reynolds family until 1868 when she left the convent and was never seen or heard from again.

On Ephriam's bookshelves were five thick books listing the rosters of every unit that fought at Gettysburg. Anne opened up the first volume and searched for the Fourteenth Tennessee Regiment, finally finding it in the third volume.

She called for Gretchen. "Do you remember Jeanie ever mentioning where she came from?" Gretchen had a good memory for long past. Many times she couldn't remember what she did a day or two ago. Also, as a pastor's wife, she long ago mastered the ability to remember facts and faces. "As I recall she came to Philadelphia as a slave girl. She was born in Louisiana, I do remember that." Anne made sure not to mention Tennessee; she didn't want to influence Gretchen's recollections. "I don't know where she was before, but I remember her master loaned her out." She kept thinking and Anne kept quiet. "I think Ephriam got a letter from a family she had stayed with. It's probably here somewhere; Ephriam never threw letters away." Anne got prepared for yet another search. "Tell Mary to get in here; it's time to find another needle in a haystack."

They searched for two days. Finally tucked inside a book about Tennessee Walking Horses was an old, yellowed and crudely written letter still in the envelope. It was addressed to *"Efrum Burnhartir."* Anne squinted to read the faded return address. She walked over to the window to get as much sunlight on it as possible. Gretchen said, "Ephriam wanted to buy one of those horses for his father to ride because they are known for being gentle animals." Anne responded while trying her best to make out the sender's name. "That's nice; Mary, try to make out this name and address."

Mary didn't need glasses yet; the two old women had been using them for years. "The problem is there are a lot of thumbprints on the return address, but it looks to me that the name is E. Keener." Gretchen shouted, "That's it! Ernie and Sarah Keener! That's who Jeanie lived with before she came to Philadelphia!"

Anne opened up the Gettysburg book to the pages listing the Fourteenth Tennessee Regiment members. Mary asked, "Have you discovered something new?" Anne didn't answer, she couldn't reveal to Mary she was investigating the murderous Jeanie Belvoir, the same Jeanie Belvoir who had held her in her arms and rocked her to sleep so many times.

Corporal Ernest Keener! Anne jumped to her feet; she wanted to blurt out the name. The unsigned letter simply said, *"I wil look fr one and lit yu no cheap."* Anne fell back into Ephriam's stuffed chair. She needed to sleep; she would stay there for the night. The next day Dominique visited. Anne told her about the recent discovery. "I am curious whether Corporal Keener was a victim or a willing conspirator." Dominique said, "What does the book say happened to Corporal Keener?" Anne hadn't recovered from seeing his name to read anything further. She looked up the regiment and his name once again. "It says '*Killed July 4, 63.*'" Dominique said, "I believe that answers your question." Anne was glad for Dominique and her talent for logical conclusions. Then again; she had an edge; she was an angel.

Dominique said, "What you really need to find is the note that Frank Herr had put in the cross. That piece of paper contained his precise prediction. That's what Jeanie wants;

she wants that note." Anne said, "But Ephriam says in his diary that he destroyed that piece of paper." Dominique said, "I don't believe he destroyed the note. It is the very information the virgin needs to know to be protected!" Hearing that shocked Anne; she never thought of that possibility. Anne wondered how the girl would get the message, whatever it is. Dominique smiled. "Anne, you need to find the note and then have faith!" Anne said, "I have the faith sister, but I am an old woman. I'll be dead. How will she get the message then?" Dominique had the answer. "Remember the shepherd with that one single lost lamb? Find the note and God will tell you what to do with it."

†

Chapter 27

1905

The message

Anne's biggest challenge was keeping the message, whatever it is, from Jeanie. Finding out what was written on that piece of paper had motivated Jeanie for all these years to threaten Ephriam, to hold Mary hostage, to cause Anne's possession, and to murder Ernie Keener, Frank Herr and other innocent people. She hoped she would be able to decipher the note and then have faith that the message will be delivered at the crucial time in the future.

She sat for hours in the study and also relaxed under the large trees in the back yard. She took the long walks she enjoyed so much. She prayed. She prayed everyday, and at church, feeling closer to God, she prayed some more. She searched her soul for the answer to the most important question she had ever asked; where was the note with this message from God?

Gretchen said, "Anne I think I have placed too much of a burden on you. I must ask for your forgiveness." Anne's reply was typical. "Nonsense, I'm just fine. I'm perhaps taking it more seriously than I thought I would, but I'll get through it. Mary and I will be done with the work soon."

Gretchen hoped that when that time came her sister-in-law would travel with her to Philadelphia for visiting, shopping, and a trip to the seashore for much needed rest. Anne was very receptive to the suggestion. "After that, I will be going back home to the North land. My husband misses me, and I miss him, my children, and my grandchildren."

She had dozed off in the stuffed chair when a loud noise entered the window from the outside. A full load of large logs had fallen off a wagon on Main Street just in front of the house, causing the windows to shake and the large cross hanging on the wall to fall to the floor. Startled, she walked over to re-hang the cross when she noticed a small section on the back covered with glued paper. She went to peel the paper away; it was so brittle that it just disintegrated. There was a small square that had been cut open and then put back into place. She picked up a letter opener from Ephriam's desk and pried off the wooden lid to the small section.

Inside the cross was a very small, one-inch square, hollowed out section. She removed the tightly wrapped piece of paper and slowly and gently unfolded it. The paper was in remarkably good condition; it looked like it was antiquarian quality, possibly what ancient scrolls were written on. Her heart was beating rapidly; she knew what she had discovered.

She read it slowly and carefully, and then she read it again. *"Know the links and save them to seven of the 21st, then rattle, then conception."* She put the note inside the pages of Ephriam's large, thick leather bound Bible. His grandfather had given it to him the day he was ordained. It was the Bible he took to the pulpit every Sunday during all those forty-four years he served St. Luke's Lutheran Church. She decided to hurry to Dominique and get her interpretation of what the message meant and her advice on what she should do with it.

When she arrived at the cottage two priests and three nuns met her. They were standing on the porch in quiet discussion. The older priest asked, "Ma'am, may I help you?" Anne said, "I'm here to see my friend, Sister Dominique." The younger priest said, "I'm sorry, Sister Dominique passed away early this morning."

Anne was devastated. She had become very fond of the nun and had depended on her for guidance. "Did she die peacefully?" The older priest said she had just died of old age. One of the nuns asked, "Is your name Anne Krieg?" Anne said, "Why yes, I'm Anne Krieg." The nun went into the cottage and returned with a note in a sealed envelope addressed "*To Anne Krieg.*" Anne opened it and read, *"Swim in the warm water, and you will always be close to Ephriam."*

That evening after supper, Anne, Gretchen, and Mary took the buggy and traveled the two miles to Lake Stamen. As rays of the setting sun reflected off the lake, the three women got undressed and waded into the water. Mary exclaimed, "It's so warm!"

They frolicked; it was a joy for the three of them. While in the water they felt as if they didn't have a care in the world. They felt good about everything, unburdened, relieved of the toil of everyday living.

For Anne it was especially rewarding. She was sharing good times with her brother's family, complying with Dominique's last wish for her, and at last uncovering the mysteries that abound in the village of Hamlin.

By the spring of 1906 Anne and Mary finished their work sorting and cataloguing Ephriam's papers. Most of his books were donated to the county library; his professional books were given to the Lutheran Seminary. His letters and other papers were presented to the county historical society.

Mary decided to keep her father's Bible. She placed it

in a small cedar wooden box she bought from a bookbinder. When Mary died years later she instructed in her will that the Bible be given to the descendents of Billy Denton.

The Bible became a family treasure. The Dentons owed Ephriam Bernharter their very existence. He had prayed for the family patriarch and saved his life.

✝

Chapter 28

1906

Anne and Balair's reunion

Anne was sitting at the backyard picnic table shelling peas when he showed up. Facing away from the house, she looked up and saw him standing in the path leading to the grape arbor. She could smell him; the putrid odor overcame the normal freshness of the air. She didn't remember meeting him in Harrisburg all those years ago. She had read Ephriam's description of him in his diary and was surprised how accurate it was. "He was dressed in black, a black cape with a red lining, and a black top hat. He looked to be about fifty years old; had a beaked nose, black rotten teeth, and smelled of urine and sweat." She noticed that he certainly had not aged; she remembered that Dominique told her demons don't age. She noticed too that his feet were about twelve inches off the ground and that his body seemed to be on the verge of turning a glowing red. Clearly, he wasn't a man; he was a demon. He reminded her of a thespian; he had a strong and forceful voice with exact phrasing. She watched the freak's eyes become pink while his pupils turned blood red; she noticed the same blue smoke that came from Daytrin's ears, nose and mouth.

He seemed anxious to speak to her. "I see you're now an old lady; old and dried up. I think I'll fuck you anyway." She turned to make sure Gretchen and Mary had left for their church meeting. "I wouldn't lie with you, it would be much worse than lying with a dog. You are not human, why would I want to lay with such a vile creature?" He began to laugh. "You're still feisty, being an old nag hasn't tamed you after all these years with your crazy husband making you do wild things."

She walked by him to the end of the back yard. He followed. "Annie, I think the time has come for you to do some work for me." She looked him in the eye. "My name isn't Annie, and I'm not doing any work for you!" He displayed his confidence with a sneer. "Annie, I own you, I am the one who commands you." She said, "You don't own me, you think you own me, you put Satan inside me years ago, but my brother sucked and blew your despicable Satan's presence from me." He laughed because he didn't believe her. "Annie, you are a good liar." He snapped his fingers, attempting to put her in a trance. Instead she walked over to him and slapped his face. He snapped his fingers again. She spit in his face. Then he used some force. He swung his arm across her head and shoulders and knocked her to the ground. "I possess you and I'm going to destroy you." He had cut her lip; she was spitting blood. "You don't possess me, and I'm going to have *you* destroyed."

She screamed as loud as she could. "Satan, your demon Balair has failed you, he has allowed Billy Denton to be healed. He has allowed the links to remain unbroken. He has failed to tell Jeanie." He kept snapping his fingers frantically with no results. He was forced to concede that Satan no longer dwelled inside her. He yelled; "Shut up old lady!" She was still lying on the ground when he walked over to her and kicked her in her side, and then again. She was surprised how little strength he had. While suffering only slight pain from his weak attempt at physical abuse, she began to recite her prayer. *"Our Father who art in Heaven, hallowed be thy name."* Balair placed his hands over his ears and screamed; "Stop!" She kept praying; *"Thine kingdom come, thy will be done."* He yelled some more. "Stop! I demand you stop!" She screamed, "You fool, you didn't even know Ephriam sucked Satan from me years ago in the safe zone! You are worthless to Satan, and he will never forgive you!" She kept up her tirade. "Satan, judge him here and now, for he has been exposed. He is a failure."

He countered with just another desperate accusation: "You are a liar!" She had more to tell Satan. "Your Balair is so stupid he thinks he can harm me; I am a woman who has been saved by Jesus Christ, I have a profound faith in him. I am not tempted by your evil, surely not by this wicked incompetent." He had begun to shake, reaching inside for words to express his contempt for her. He was beginning to get scared; the words were not forthcoming. Anne kept up her prayer. *"On Earth as it is in Heaven. Give us this day our daily bread and forgive us our trespasses as we forgive those who trespass against us."* She was getting louder now. "Balair, you are my trespasser, and now I have told Satan. I was freed of his horrible spirit, my faith prevents you from harming me!" Just like Daytrin, he was starting to panic. She kept praying. *"And lead us not into temptation, but deliver us from evil."* She kept her eyes on him. "I've been delivered from evil Balair." She noticed that now he too had become quiet and calm. *"For thine is the kingdom, and the power, and the glory, forever and ever, Amen."*

She walked over to the picket fence and tore a loose board from the support, pulling the nails with it. Balair had underestimated her. She was an old woman, but she had been a crusader for justice, an activist, she was a veteran fierce fighter. Her sudden burst of extraordinary strength that the Holy Spirit was giving her through faith surprised her; it felt good to experience the stamina she had years ago. He had dropped his head in defeat, and she took advantage of it. She used all the strength she could muster to hit him with the board. Startled, he looked up at her as she hit him again. "Evidently Satan is going to spare you, but I'm not going to." He yowled, "You crazy woman, you can't destroy me!" When she hit him again he staggered backwards, finally falling to the ground. She was gasping for breath but found the energy to hit his face again. She saw no marks, not from the board's impact or the nails piercing his ashen skin. She was beginning to sense she had met her match. Was it time to flee? There was nowhere on Earth she could go to hide from this miserable creature! Just then he began to vomit, the putrid smelling liquid came out of his mouth like a geyser in a continuous flow reaching fifteen feet into the air. Anne staggered back to get away from the matter as it started to fall back down to the ground. She watched the geyser of vomit go on for over ten minutes while the demon's body kept shrinking smaller and smaller, shriveling like a grape becoming a raisin. Exhausted, she went back into the house to wash up. When she returned all that remained was a patch of dead grass where he had lied. Finally Satan had put an end to his existence.

   She knelt and prayed some more. Attempts to destroy her failed; there was an absence of original sin in her. Satan had heard Anne's shouts.

✝

Chapter 29

1992

Elizabeth solves the mystery

In 1992 David Denton, Billy Denton's great-grandson, died. He was eighty-five years old. In his will he left the Bernharter Bible to his daughters Sarah and Rebecca.

Sarah was a world traveler. She engaged in adventures that most members of the family looked at unfavorably. She wanted to be an actress and frequented the theater districts of New York and London. She met the wrong kind of men and eventually adopted their primary bad habit of living in a drunken stupor most of their waking hours, including the times that parts to plays were being given out.

Rebecca, on the other hand, was pretty, small and fragile and was interested in things that kept her in the home; she liked to cook, sew, and mend, and tend to the garden in the back yard.

Laura Denton, David's widow, and the mother of Sarah and Rebecca, decided that Rebecca would get the Bible. She didn't trust Sarah to safeguard the heirloom. Sarah didn't think her mother's decision was quite fair. She felt she was responsible enough to be entrusted with it. Laura thought Sarah would eventually pawn it. Laura won the argument.

Rebecca didn't want to go through life having her sister angry with her. She decided to offer a compromise. She would give the Bible to her son Nathan. She was sure that Nathan would safeguard it; he was a high school history teacher and had interest in the Denton family history and pride in his family's heritage.

Rebecca remembered that her father had always kept the Bible atop his bedroom chest of drawers. While she was growing up she would go into her parent's bedroom and put her nose against the cedar box and breathe in the wonderful smell. She didn't dare open the box or ask permission to hold the old book. She was in awe whenever she was reminded that this was the same Bible that legendary Reverend Ephriam Bernharter, the pastor who saved her ancestor's life, used to preach the Gospel.

When Rebecca gave Nathan the Bible he did like family members before him; he kept it in the cedar box, afraid to hold it. Nathan appreciated his daughter Elizabeth's interest the Bible. Ten years earlier when she was writing a tenth grade report about something interesting her family owned, the only possible subject of her paper was the family Bible. In her report she mentioned that she hoped someday her Grandmother would inherit it and give it to her. Nathan was emphatic; "If you ever have the opportunity to hold it, take it out of the box carefully, and while turning the pages make sure you don't tear them, and please don't drop it."

When Nathan took possession of it, Elizabeth was the first person to open the Bible in many years. She found the note. She found that piece of paper that Anne Krieg placed inside the thick leather bound Bible in 1905.

After graduating from high school she enrolled at the local community college so she could be close to home. She chose, as did her father before her, American history as her major. Elizabeth was a brilliant young woman. She had been born with a heart condition. What she lacked in physical stamina she compensated with boundless energy as a student. She read constantly. She joined formal and informal discussion groups. She and friends talked about philosophy, different religions, cultures, and odd theories.

She studied Carl Schurz, mostly because of her being told while she was growing up about his legendary visit to Hamlin. She never found anything to substantiate that claim. There is no mention of a ride North in the official records of the Civil War, and Schurz never mentioned it in his memoirs. During the summer break after her freshman year, she began studying the Denton family tree. After finding out about Billy Denton and his service in the Civil War, she became convinced that Schurz did indeed bring her injured ancestor to Hamlin.

She asked her minister Reverend Trembor, the current pastor of St. Luke's Church, if there were any records of Reverend Bernharter's sermons. The jolly, short and round elderly clergyman, with thin snow-white hair, was well aware of Elizabeth's voracious appetite for researching just about any subject she had the slightest interest in. He leaned back in his old, creaky wooden office chair. "I have never seen any; we do have records of guest pastors though, would that help you? She never let slip by the opportunity to see old records. "It might help, can I look at the file?"

She searched the list of guest preachers during the years that Ephriam served the church. Of course Luther Bernharter was listed many times. There were few others. At Ephriam's ordination service a Revered Frank Herr from the Philadelphia Lutheran Seminary was a guest.

She asked Reverend Trembor if he ever heard of Frank Herr. "Oh my goodness yes! He was a professor at the seminary and later studied ancient scrolls. He wrote many articles that questioned and reaffirmed our faith at the same time." Elizabeth was fascinated. "I wonder why he came to Hamlin?" Trembor replied, "I remember someone telling me he was friends with the elder Bernharter. I think Ephriam Bernharter had him as an instructor in seminary, and later they became close friends."

Elizabeth visited the Philadelphia library to try and find something, anything that Reverend Herr had written. She found only three different articles he wrote for an alternative theology magazine.

She was sitting in the massive library at one of the large oak tables, reading copies of the three articles when a man sat down across the table. "Elizabeth, I can probably help you with any questions about Reverend Herr." Startled, she looked up at the strange and different looking man sitting there. He was wearing an immaculately clean and tailored blue suit, a white shirt with starched color, and a maroon necktie with a perfect Windsor knot. He was perhaps thirty years old, with a full head of straight blonde hair, parted on the side and combed over. "Do you work here? How do you know I'm researching Frank Herr?" Smiling, he told her he was a research assistant for the library.

She welcomed the help. "All I found about Herr were these three articles, which to be perfectly honest with you, make no sense to me. Hey, what's your name?"

He chuckled, his face wearing a broad, perfectly innocent smile. "Ok, my name is Michael. Now what information about your family are you searching for?" She began to tell him about the local legend that General Carl Schurz brought her injured ancestor to Hamlin for treatment after the battle of Gettysburg.

Michael's look on his face turned serious. He said, "That's true! I can't tell you everything, but I can tell you that an ancestor of yours is going to die at the exact same time a descendent of yours becomes pregnant by Immaculate Conception." Elizabeth's jaw dropped. "Hey, who the hell are you?" He said, "I told you, I'm a research assistant."

Elizabeth, feeling very uncomfortable, resumed reading the three articles.

"I thought you wanted answers. Does it really matter who I am?" She stopped reading again and asked, "Ok, tell me what you know about Frank Herr." He was eager to tell; he was behaving like someone preparing to talk some gossip over a backyard fence. "After he retired as a professor of theology, he moved to Canada and started to research these ancient scrolls that some institute up there dug up somewhere. Then he got murdered!"

That got Elizabeth's attention. "Did they ever find out who murdered him?" Michael replied, "No the killer was never caught. There might have been more than one." He continued, "He had written these three controversial articles; at the time nobody knew what happened to all his research papers, thousands of pages. It had been suspected for years that a minister who had visited him just before he was killed stole them. Eventually the minister's family donated them to the Seminary in Philadelphia."

Elizabeth confessed, "My family has that minister's leather bound Bible. I found an old note in it. I think I figured out what it means. It predicts exactly what you've told me."

Michael said, "Elizabeth, write on the back of the note what you have discovered. It's important that the links to the chain not be broken!" She said, "I haven't discovered anything, you just finished telling me facts that I assume are true; you seem pretty convinced they're true. Either that or you're a pretty good salesman or con-artist."

Michael said, "Read what Herr writes in paragraph 7 of article 2. Believe it, it's the truth. Believe what he has written there. It was taken from the scrolls. Make it part of your faith."

Elizabeth said, "OK, I'll read it. Right now I need to use the ladies' room." When she came back a few minutes later Michael was gone. Herr spent years translating the scrolls and interpreting what he believed their passages meant. In paragraph 7 of article 2 he quoted a passage from the scrolls. *"When the judgment day cometh, and the saved are resurrected, the Lord will ask, 'Where is thy hallowed ground, thy place where ye have made a difference while living? For ye shall surely have a place in Heaven, and the maid who lies there to guard it and keep it holy, she too shall rise into the clouds to be with the Lord.'"*

When she returned from Philadelphia Elizabeth told Nathan and Katie, "If anything happens to me before I get married, promise me you'll have me buried at Gettysburg. Dad, you're a veteran; I can be buried there if I'm unmarried. I want to be there with the thousands of soldiers who gave their lives to save our country." Nathan said, "You're too young to be thinking about dying, but you are a special kid. Your mind is always working; it's like a time bomb, always ticking."

"Mom, promise me." Katie said yes.

Eight months later while she was watching television, Elizabeth lost consciousness and died of heart failure.

She was buried at Gettysburg National Cemetery in the annex, mostly alongside veterans of the Vietnam War and their family members.

Chapter 30

2007

Births and Deaths

Ephriam Bernharter born 1819. Died 1905. Age 86.
Gretchen Stanton Bernharter born 1823. Died 1910. Age 87.
Mary Bernharter born 1843. Died 1924. Age 81.

Anne Bernharter Krieg born 1820. Died 1911. Age 91.

Billy Denton born 1838. Died 1901.
Billy & Martha Denton's son Billy Jr. born 1868. Died 1942.
Billy Jr. & Amanda Denton's son Adam born 1889. Died 1968.
Adam & Victoria Denton's son David born 1907. Died 1992.
David & Laura Denton's daughter Sarah born 1925. Died 2000.
David & Laura Denton's daughter Rebecca born 1926. Died 2007.
Frederick & Rebecca (Denton) Keller's son Nathan born 1944.
Nathan & Katie Keller's daughter Elizabeth born 1966. Died 1993.
Nathan & Katie Keller's son Charles born 1967.
Charles & Sandra Keller's daughter Julia born 1987.

† Chapter 31

2007

The Irony

On a quiet spring evening, Katie was attending a church meeting in Jenkinstown, Nathan sat in the small restaurant along the highway that ran from Franklinsburg to Jenkinstown, just three miles from Hamlin. While visiting Elizabeth's grave a few months earlier, he was perusing the thousands of books in an old bookstore when he happened upon a three-volume set of books, their mint condition and shiny oxblood color attracting him. He bought the set for twenty dollars. The three volumes contained the memoirs of Carl Schurz, published in 1908. While Katie attended her meeting he began reading the first volume while enjoying a cup coffee. As expected, this high school history teacher enjoyed reading accounts of American's past, especially the very words of the men and women who made our history.

Thirty years earlier, in 1969, he had sat in the very same restaurant, just ten feet away, having breakfast with 3 year old Elizabeth before traveling to the army five miles West to get copies of his military orders sending him to Germany. Katie, Elizabeth and Charles would be going along.

GARY LUDWIG

Naturally Nathan had never stopped missing Elizabeth. Now, fifteen years after her death, the idle days of summer vacation gave him time for fresh reflection; he thought about her more than usual this time of year.

He knew a little about Carl Schurz; most people never heard of him. The man never enjoyed much fame despite his achievements and contributions. Nathan remembered while growing up hearing the old people of Hamlin talk about the rainy night that Major General Carl Schurz and his entourage rode into the village on a secret mission the day after the Battle of Gettysburg. Supposedly he brought a wounded soldier named Billy Denton home.

Because Nate was a Denton, he naturally had a keen interest in the local legend, planning someday to spend time tracing the origins of it.

Nate took a sip of his coffee and opened up volume one and began to read. The German-American legislator, reformer, and journalist, was born in 1829 in Erftstadt, Germany! Nathan couldn't believe his eyes. How ironic! Schurz was born in the town that Nate, Katie, Elizabeth and Charles, had lived in for almost two years! Then he realized he was sitting ten feet from the spot he and Elizabeth sat while having breakfast over thirty years earlier!

These weren't Nate's only surprises. More was to come.

While he read he learned that Schurz was educated at the University of Bonn, he became involved in the rebellion of 1848-49, fled the country when the revolt was put down and then helped spring revolutionary Gottfried Kinkel from the Spandau Prison. In 1852 he came to the United States, practiced law, gave anti-slavery speeches, and campaigned for Abraham Lincoln. After serving as Ambassador to Spain he was appointed a Major General in the Union Army. He died in New York on May 14, 1906 after a post war career in journalism and politics.

Later that evening, before he could tell Katie about Schurz, he was stunned when she said, "Let's go to Gettysburg Sunday, I'd like to visit Elizabeth's grave."

That Sunday was a beautiful summer day, with plenty of sunshine, moderate temperature, and a slight breeze to aid the comfort of everyone. After Nate and Katie trimmed around the tombstone, Nathan looked up and noticed a large monument, its inscription he had never taken the time to read before. They walked the 100 feet or so West to get to it, walked around to its front, and read the incredible inscription. *"Here, just East about thirty-five yards, was the field headquarters of Major General Carl Schurz!"*

Elizabeth's grave lay at the very same spot, give or take a few feet, where General Schurz's tent was pitched; it was exactly where Schurz and Captain Denton stood together and where Denton got wounded.

Nathan knew there was a significance to all this, but he didn't know what it was. Katie didn't share his melancholy feelings. Although she was devastated when Elizabeth died, she had taken her death much better than Nathan ever did. "I don't think it's a coincidence. I think Schurz is watching over our daughter." Katie tried her best to be sensitive and sympathetic. She believed in God, Heaven, life after death, and all those things Christians are taught to believe. She felt she had enough faith. "Why would he watch over Elizabeth?" Nate responded, "Maybe she's watching the ground where he spent the most critical hours in his life."

Katie was willing to admit what Nathan was saying made sense. "I guess if you believe in God, then you should believe stuff like that happens." While they were sitting in a coffee shop having lunch he asked Katie the question he feared would trouble him for the rest of his life. "Why Elizabeth? Why is he watching over her?" Why is she watching him, or the monument, or the ground?

Nathan decided he would go through Elizabeth's personal items the family had kept in a chest of drawers in the attic. It was painful, but he forced himself to search for clues to this mysterious association between Carl Schurz, Billy Denton, and his dead daughter Elizabeth. He never found any information that connected her to Schurz or the legend that hovered over Denton family households for 144 years.

†

Chapter 32

2007

The annunciation

It was a sunny and crisp winter Sunday morning when the congregation of St. Luke's Lutheran Church gathered for worship and to celebrate Reverend Anthony Gabriela's anniversary as pastor.

He was a tall thin man with black hair and olive skin. His father was Italian, a Roman Catholic. His mother, of German descent, came from a family of devout Lutherans. Anthony received his calling from God when he was fourteen years of age. After his ordination in 1996 he served as an associate pastor at a large Philadelphia church until he was called by St. Luke's. He was a gentle, quiet man who was very popular with church members. He comforted the sick and elderly and was an advocate of the church's youth. His skills at marriage and family counseling, and his comforting words during times of bereavement help solidify him as a powerful influence in the community. His reserved nature didn't affect his sermons; he preached with a loud resonant voice and wasn't afraid to give his opinion or apply the Lord's teachings to sensitive and controversial issues.

He decided to preach on this Sunday of celebration using

Reverend Ephriam Bernharter's old Bible. The day before he had removed the old book from the antique wooden box it was always kept in. It was still in excellent condition; it had been printed in the nineteenth century on quality, acid resistant paper, hand bound, and encased in the splendid natural leather cover.

From the pulpit he talked about the former pastor. "He greatly influenced this congregation by leading its members through the joys and tribulations that are part of life. We owe him a great deal for helping to establish the foundation that St. Luke's Lutheran Church stands firm on." Then he made an announcement that shocked Nate and Katie Keller. "Holding Reverend Bernharter's Bible, and reading today's lesson from it, is a sacred honor to me. Having this treasured Bible here on the pulpit was made possible by Elizabeth Keller, who presented it to the church only one month before she passed away at a very young age in 1989." Nathan was stunned; Katie wept and knelt to pray. They had never missed the Bible. Elizabeth never told any family member she gave the Bible to the church.

Reverend Gabriela gave his lesson; he read from the Book of Revelation about the end of the world and how Satan's rule through man will be destroyed by the Savior. He spoke of the Great Tribulation and the campaign of Armageddon. Then he began his sermon about the Second Coming of Jesus Christ and the restoration of peace to the world. He read from the old Bernharter Bible about the Lord's 1,000 year reign and God's final judgment over Satan.

When he turned a page, he noticed a yellowed piece of paper and began stuttering and ad libbing while he read what was scrawled on it; *"Know the links and save them to seven of the 21st, then rattle, then conception."* He paused; the church became very quiet, no longer filled with the compelling sound of his voice. He turned the piece of paper over and read what was neatly written on the back; it was obvious it had been written much later. *"Billy Denton was saved, and each descendent takes us one step closer to the second miracle birth in the seventh year of the 21st century; 2007. A family member will die that year on the same day the virgin will conceive by the hand of God."*

Gabriela didn't resume preaching. He turned to his left and walked to the front of the altar and fell to his knees. *"We ask for thy mercy dear God. The Second Coming of your Son is at hand!"* Cries came from members of the congregation. Most knelt and prayed aloud, causing a loud murmuring from so many individual prayers echoing in the sanctuary, punctuated by weeping and the crying out by the people who never imagined they would be alive when Christ returned to Earth. Nathan and Katie were praying for Elizabeth.

Suddenly the sky darkened and a strong wind picked up; heavy rain began falling accompanied by thunder and lightning. Two elders went to the altar and helped the weeping pastor to his office where they lay him on his couch.

Only one person got up to leave during the confusion and disorder. She was a small, pretty African-American girl who had attended Sunday services periodically in the past. She always sat in the back pew. Nobody seemed to know her. Someone had mentioned earlier that her name was Jeanie.

†

Chapter 33

2007

The conception

Julia Keller, Nate and Katie's granddaughter usually wore her long chestnut brown hair in a ponytail or pinned up in a casual way so that curls were always falling randomly alongside her face. She never liked to wear make-up like most of her friends did; she had natural beauty, near perfect facial features, perfect teeth, slender shape, and a broad smile to augment her sense of humor.

She was working hard to earn her bachelor's degree from a small college in Maryland and then planned to attend law school. She never had a steady boyfriend, the only dating she did was for school dances, the senior prom, and when she was homecoming queen and needed an escort.

Recently she had met Jim Sanders at college. She felt comfortable being with him. She appreciated that he was shy and a little naïve about girls. She didn't want a serious relationship at this stage in her young life. Her goals and the hard work that went with them were her priority. She wanted to be a defense attorney, maybe work for a social service agency providing legal aid to the poor.

Julia appreciated how deep her family's roots were in

the community and how those roots nourished her personal identity. Her father Charles, Nathan and Katie's son, was a successful house builder, her mother the school librarian.

She had volunteered to spend the summer watching her gravely ill great-grandmother Rebecca who was bedridden in a downstairs room in Nathan and Katie's house. Rebecca, now eighty-one years old, had suffered several strokes. She weighted less than ninety-five pounds and slept most of the time.

Nathan had refused to put her into a nursing home. In addition to his and Katie's caring for her, visiting nurses and housekeeping aids made daily house calls administering medications, monitoring her vital signs, and providing personal care. When she had her first stroke at age seventy-four the doctors told Nate she wouldn't survive the next inevitable stroke. But Rebecca had hung on to life.

Julia's helping with the old woman was appreciated, and it was also a good arrangement for Julia. While helping her family it also gave her opportunity to read and do advanced study work while sitting bedside. It enabled Rebecca to have companionship, and when she was feeling strong enough, to tell Julia stories about how it was to live in Hamlin in years past.

At the very same time the chaos was taking place at the church, Julia was trying to take a nap on the stuffed chair next to Rebecca's bed. It had been a bad night for the old woman. Julia had been awake most of the night. She got up and went over to the window to lower it, concerned that the strong wind was going to blow the rain inside. Rebecca's horrible, loud moans were overwhelming the sound of the thunder and the hard rain hitting the tin roof.

Julia did finally doze off. It was then that Rebecca stopped breathing. An hour later she awoke and looked at the old lady's still body and realized that she was dead.

Julia was scared, she had only seen dead people at funerals; she didn't know what to do. She was horror-struck. Pacing from the kitchen to the parlor, she paused to look into Rebecca's room each time she passed it. She felt helpless; she finally concluded she should try to stay calm and wait for her grandparents to come home from church. She knew her grandfather would take charge and do all the appropriate and necessary things that needed to be done.

Unexpectedly the corpse left out a death rattle - the involuntary contraction of her vocal chords. "EEEEEPPPP-PHHHHHRRRRRIIIIIAAAAAMMMMM!" The crying out terrified her. She didn't expect anything but cold dead silence from a corpse.

She was pacing around in the parlor, when all of a sudden, she felt faint. She fell down and managed to get back up on her feet. She staggered across the room while trying to stay standing. She fell down again, this time knocking over the end table next to the couch and breaking a delicate antique lamp. She once again managed to get to her feet; this time she extended her arms for guidance and protection like a blind person or a sleepwalker. It was no use, for she was too dizzy; she lay on the floor next to the couch and closed her eyes while feeling her entire body get warm. She felt a horrible pain in her abdomen; she was sure she was going to die. Enduring the agony brought her to tears. She had curled up into the fetal position. The pain began to pass after about 5 minutes. Exhausted, she fell into a deep sleep.

The heavy rain continued to fall. Nathan and Katie were due home but the storm had knocked down power lines on the highway, closing it to all traffic.

Now somebody was knocking loudly on the door of the house. The knocking got louder, but Julia didn't awake. It got louder still. But the caller got no response.

The caller shouted so loud the house shook. "Whoever heard the call for Ephriam come to me now!"

The loud demand was deep and masculine, certainly not the voice you would expect from a small black woman, her clothing completely soaked from the rain.

Julia stayed asleep.

The hideous voice became deeper and more distorted. The caller's appearance started to change, from that of a small pretty black woman to a twisted and warped creature with scales beginning to protrude from her skin. Her feet and legs began curling, becoming webbed and wing like. Her arms were getting shorter, and her fingers were becoming claws. She took on a slight red glow. Her face was being re-formed into that of a serpent, and when she called out once again blue smoke came from her mouth. "Whoever heard that call for Ephriam come to me now!" She caused the house to shake again

Enraged, she ran to the front yard, prepared to shout until the house fell to the ground. "Whoever heard the call for Ephriam come to me now!"

Jeanie had failed once again. Julia had conceived in an immaculate way.

Suddenly Satan, infuriated by this final, devastating failure, roared from Hell, shaking the Earth under the Keller house. Jeanie fell to the ground and held her clawed hands over her ears, trying to escape Satan's horrible howls. She began to glow a bright red and then she burst into flames; the heat was intense. She lied in the mud screaming and moaning while she burned; the ground under her began to sink; raindrops turned to steam as they pelted her. Soon her charred corpse began to cool. Lying in the muddy sinkhole, it melted, turned liquid and seeped into the ground.

When Julia recovered and got to her feet, the house was dark, electric service had been lost. She staggered to the front parlor window and noticed there weren't any cars traveling on the street. Worried, she decided to call her grandfather's cell phone. "Grandpa, grandma has passed away. Could you please come home right away? The storm has caused a large sinkhole in front of the house. It's filling up with water."

Nathan and Katie finally made it home. Rebecca's funeral was a few days later.

In later years when they visited the hallowed ground in Gettysburg, Nathan and Katie felt they were not only visiting their daughter's grave, they were sure they were visiting an Angel that had been sent to them.

A month after Rebecca's funeral Julia consented to accompany Jim Sanders on a two-year church mission trip to Africa rather than return to college. There they would not need to hide her pregnancy.

Reverend Gabriela counseled them before they left. He told them they would have to accept their relationship as a very special one. He told Julia she would be giving birth to a baby boy.

In her letter to Reverend Gabriela announcing the birth, Julia said she and Jim feel blessed. She described how native women were attending to her and the baby, and how the women in the village seemed angel like.

Later Julia and Jim were married in Kenya.

She wrote in her diary; *"It is the end of the beginning. It is the beginning of the end. Hope has no more purpose, for the time is surely here now."*

Printed in the United States
124603LV00002B/376-399/P